LOVE HAS SILENT WINGS
by
Vera Holding and Joe Christy

Debbie Mills was only seventeen and still in high school, but because her father operated the Twin Lakes Airport in Kansas and the motherless girl had practically grown up there, she was as much at home in the air as most girls are in cars or on bicycles on the ground. Although not yet old enough to operate a glider commercially for pay, Debbie was already an expert, and was in love with Don Carver in part at least because he shared her feeling for the open spaces of the sky.

Therefore the threat that the City Council might not renew her father's lease to operate the airport was a crushing blow to Debbie; more so because it was spearheaded by Don's parents.

A Teen-Age Romance about one of the nation's most popular new pastimes.

LOVE HAS SILENT WINGS

LOVE HAS SILENT WINGS

by

VERA HOLDING AND JOE CHRISTY

Alouette Romance
By
Sharon Publications, Inc.
Closter, NJ

Copyright © MCMLXIII by Arcadia House
Published by
Sharon Publications Inc.
Closter, N.J. 07624
Printed in the U.S.A.
Cover illustrations by Mel Greifinger
ISBN 0-89531-148-8

LOVE HAS SILENT WINGS

CHAPTER I

It wheeled in great joyous circles, far above the Kansas plain. It was a graceful, silent thing, more bird than machine. For a sailplane has no engine. Its whispering flight is born of the undisciplined wind.

In its narrow cockpit, Debbie Mills tossed her head in exultation and flung her buoyant craft closer and closer to the face of a summer thunderhead. She felt a part of all this; light, giddy, free and as undisciplined as the wind which bore her. The thunderhead became a white charger racing against the wind, and on his back sat Don . . . handsome Don Carver, in his eyes that squinting, smiling look which held her like a caress.

The storm cloud grumbled a lofty threat as if to remind her that Don would be coming for his flying lesson soon. To hold the image of the white charger a minute longer in her heart, she held her breath, then dodged away, banking steeply.

Oh, maybe Don would already be there when she landed. Maybe she could jump into his arms.

She couldn't get home fast enough. Hurry, hurry, her heart beat out the rhythm, as she slid over a precipice of air and swooped earthward on laughter-silvered wings.

Moments later, she coasted over the airport fence, the wind's astonished whistle following her from the high places. She ignored the long concrete runway and touched down softly in the grass beside the hangar. She took in long breaths of air. She felt as if she'd been running for a long time.

The mute plane rolled but a few feet and then came to rest, balancing on its single wheel and wingtip. Debbie swung open the canopy and hopped to the ground, her heart still pounding with excitement. Aware of the two men watching from the hangar doorway, she made a little pirouette, then courtesied, laughing. Her heart began to do a steady beat now. Don hadn't arrived yet. She hadn't missed him. But now she'd have no excuse to jump into his arms. Then she smiled to herself. *There could always be another time. She could always take the glider up.* It was her very own. Happiness spread through her as she walked briskly to join the two men.

The younger of them was frowning slightly as she approached. "That was fine control handling, Deb," her father said. "Very competent. But weren't you crowding that thunderhead a bit? You know there's quite a lot of turbulance around one of those things."

That was it. *Maybe she needed to crowd Don a bit to wake him up*. Then she smiled to herself. The turbulance was all one-sided. Don hadn't seemed the least "turbulent" within or without, for that matter.

These thoughts raced through her mind, but she managed to answer her dad. "Why, Dad," she said, "I just barely stuck a wing into the rough air! I knew where it would be."

"Sure you did," he smiled, "but I wish you wouldn't cut it so closely." He shook his head and put his arm around Debbie's shoulders. "Not that I've forgotten how wings felt when *I* was seventeen." He sobered, hesitating. "When you get some time, I want to talk with you. It's important."

"Okay." It sounded grim, and the way her dad had turned abruptly and gone back inside the hangar was not like him. Bless his heart. He hadn't been like himself lately. Maybe he'd tell her what had been the matter, or why he had been worrying. She'd hurry and go see what it was he wanted.

She turned to George, the old mechanic. "Will you help me put the glider in, George? It's going to rain."

"You bet, Miss Debbie. It handled all right, didn't it?" His wind-bronzed face held pride and affection as he came toward her.

"Better than any factory-built model. You're a genius."

George ducked his head modestly. "Aw, shoot, it's only common sense." He was Debbie's slave, and they both knew it. George had worked for her father since the end of World War II. During the war, her dad and George had served together on the aircraft carrier *Enterprise*. Now, above their heads, the thunderstorm grumbled again.

"Hurry, George, or we'll get soaked!" Debbie raced to the glider and, squinting her eyes in the effort, began pushing with all her ninety-seven pounds. The sun-glow on her cheeks burned, and her long pony tail fanned out against the wind.

A couple of minutes later, they had parked Debbie's sailplane inside, between the yellow cub and Ben Mills' favorite, the green and white TriPacer. A third plane, a red Fairchild, sat behind. The Fairchild was almost as old as Debbie, but it had, under George's care, remained sound and shiny. Outside, the rain began to drum its fingers against the hangar roof.

Debbie walked back to the wide doorway to look up into the darkened sky. It was a typical July shower, made of big, hard-driving drops that would soon pass. Rain had never made her feel depressed. She wanted to run out in it, to feel its slanting lances against her face. Maybe it was because she understood about weather.

Reared motherless at the Twin Lakes Airport, she had learned about lapse rates and dew points before she could conjugate verbs. And she knew that always above the overcast, the sun still shone—that the other side of earth's misty garment was a beautiful lucent white, sequined with tiny mistbows and trimmed with cumulus lace. That was the side that fliers knew, and Debbie had flown since memory began.

Even before school age she had often accompanied her father on his charter trips, when George was not around to double as baby sitter. Buckled into the co-pilot's seat, the top of her blonde head barely level with the bottom of the window, she had spent count-less hours returning the instrument's bold stares and watched, fascinated, as raindrops struck the windshield to be shattered into minute points of light and squeezed into delicate snowflake patterns by the prop blast.

Before she had ever heard of or could ever pronounce "static electricity," she had seen its terrifying beauty as a blue and gold circle of fire haloing the spinning propeller. She had learned of "zero gravity" one stormy afternoon above the Sacramento mountains, watching her dad's sun glasses float mysteriously about the cabin. (When the plane leveled off, they had banged her on the head.)

Having been schooled on the airman's campus, which is ten miles high and a million miles wide— Debbie knew about weather and airplanes and loneliness. Oh, her dad had tried to be everything to her —mother, father, brothers and sisters which she might have had. But after all, he did have to attend to business, to make a living for them.

And there were long lonely hours, especially in the vacation periods when school was dismissed and other girls went off with their families to vacation places in the mountains, or some cool shining lake. That was the time when she realized that life might be something more than an air strip with two loving, kindly fliers whom she adored.

And then she had met Don, and the world had suddenly changed into a bright shining place where loneliness was a complete stranger.

She turned from the hangar doorway and took a tentative step toward the office. Somehow she dreaded this interview. She knew that her father had been worried for some time now, and she could hardly bear to think of anything bad ever happening to him or threatening him. Oh, well, maybe she only borrowed trouble. Maybe it only concerned Shayna Todd, her cousin, who was coming for a visit. Or maybe it was about Don Carver. Just thinking his full name made her heart begin to do a dizzy whirl again. But surely Dad wouldn't be worried about Don in any way. She put a smile on her lips and went on inside.

Her dad was working on the ledger. She leaned over his shoulder. "This is supposed to be my job, Mr. Mills."

He put his pen aside. "You've been so busy with your glider that I thought I'd help."

"I appreciate it. But I should earn my twenty a week. I'll surely be glad when I'm eighteen and air regulations will allow me to fly for pay. Then I'll deserve the title: 'partner.' "

He got to his feet, squeezing her shoulder affectionately. He was nearly forty now, but except for the bald spot showing through his brown crewcut, Debbie could detect little difference between him and the handsome Navy pilot who grinned from the old photo on her dresser. The squint lines beside his calm grey eyes were deeper, and his heavy tan failed to hide the skin coarseness that middle age brings. But she suspected that twenty years ago, his perfect nose, high cheek bones and firm chin must have combined to put her father definitely in the "squeal-bait" class. How proud she was of him: slender and erect, with no sign of an expanding waistline.

He stood now, absently studying the yellowed safety slogans tacked at random about the walls. Clearly he had something distasteful on his mind. She had to help him, bless him. He acted as if he didn't know how to begin.

"Nice rain," Debbie prompted.

"Yes, but it'll stop before Don comes for his flying lesson." He flipped through some papers on the desk.

"Don?" she repeated, making her voice sound vague, as if she were trying to place the name. "Oh, of course, I'd forgotten." She wanted to do a little dance step, her heart was doing a rhumba on its own, and she grinned impishly.

"I'll bet you had." He answered her grin by pulling her over on his lap.

She looked deep into his eyes, trying to probe out the real answers which he might be covering up. "Well, what do you think of him?"

"Well—" her dad took a deep breath—"with only three hours of dual instruction, Don wants to fly the Cub like a jet. But if I can curb his eagerness a little, he'll turn out okay."

"But how do you like him personally?" She tried to say it lightly, but she could hear the note of urgency. in her voice. She hoped her dad hadn't noticed it.

"Any boy willing to part with his jalopy in order to finance instruction is going to be a pilot." Her father grinned, adding, "I like him."

Debbie wanted to throw her arms about her dad's neck.

"Deb, would it make much difference to you if we moved away from Twin Lakes?" He didn't meet her eyes.

She could feel her nerves jump.

"What I mean is," he went on quickly, "this isn't the fanciest place in the world—that is, well, what's so special about it?" He took a match from his pocket and started chewing on it. "The city owns the land.

All we have, besides our planes, is a hangar and this dinky office, plus a four-room apartment tacked on in front."

Debbie couldn't find her voice for a moment. *Leave Twin Lakes . . . all those happy memories . . . Don. Why, it just wasn't happening. It couldn't be happening.* But she could see that her dad was waiting for her to say something.

"What's happening, Dad? What do you mean— leave Twin Lakes? Why are you holding out on me? You said that we are partners, remember?" She sprang up from his lap and began pacing back and forth, her mind and heart in a turmoil.

"The city council has refused to renew our lease." He said the words like a child who had memorized his lines. Debbie whirled and came back to him. Unbelief, shock, bewilderment and anger all boiled up inside her.

"You mean . . . But I don't understand, Dad. Do they want more rent?" It had never occurred to Debbie that this could happen.

"No," her father said. "I'm not sure what they want. Their official excuse is that I'm too conservative. The way they put it, the airport should be a progressive, newsworthy operation, buzzing with activity as it leads

Twin Lakes into the space age." He shrugged his
shoulders and sighed heavily. "But you know I get
the feeling that there's something else behind this
move of theirs."

Hot indignation began to burn inside Debbie, then
grew into seething anger as she leaned forward and
said, "It's the unfairest thing I ever heard of. You
started this airport!"

Her father doubled his fist and pounded his knee.
"It does seem strange that the city council has been
satisfied with me all these years, and now—" But
Debbie broke in. She had just thought of something.

"Don's father's on the city council! I'll bet he can
do something for us."

Her dad avoided looking at her. "I'm afraid he's
the one who did all the talking, Deb. And since he
owns the *Journal,* he can wield a big stick." He chewed
furiously on the unlighted match.

Debbie frowned. Why, it couldn't be true. Not Don's
father!

"If only," her dad resumed, "the city would sell
us this land. All three of our planes are paid for now.
I could borrow enough on them to—"

Debbie grabbed his hands in enthusiasm. "Of
course, and then we could incorporate and have a

company." But he shook his head, and her voice trailed off.

"They won't sell," he said despondently.

"We'll do something!" she declared. "We won't just quit!" Don would help them win his dad over to their side, she was confident.

Her dad's sober expression relaxed. "I knew that was what you'd say. We'll stay right here, won't we, Deb?" He squeezed her in relief.

"Roger! I have just begun to fight till I see the whites of their eyes!"

He looked at her, startled. "Who said *that*?"

She squinted thoughtfully at the ceiling. "General Custer?"

Her father laughed. "I hope not. Look what happened to him." He went to the door, still chuckling, as a transient plane taxied up to the gas pumps.

Debbie began to relax, too. As long as her dad could chuckle, things weren't too bad. Her good humor came back to the surface, and she again turned to the ledger. Don was due any minute now for his lesson. The rain was diminishing, and her heart lifted again.

There was a whole stack of gasoline invoices to be entered, but it was hard to concentrate. Her thoughts kept returning to the city council's ultimatum, and probing for the reason behind it. More than a business was threatened. This was home—the only one she could remember. Long ago, it had been someone's dream. Certainly it had been a very modest dream, but one which had sustained her mother when Debbie was a baby and the three of them had lived in back of the hangar.

Debbie would always be thankful that the dream had begun to come true before the stormy December night when Judith, her mother, had died in the wreckage of their car. Her mother had been returning from a shopping trip to Wichita. It had been Debbie's fifth Christmas.

Debbie's mother never saw the fine, smooth, runway or the beautiful green and white TriPacer, but she had known they would come, because Judith Mills believed work and faith and good humor would get almost anything.

Debbie had turned to the ledger again when George entered, wiping his hands on an oily rag. He fussed with his pipe for a minute or two before he spoke.

"Miss Debbie," he said, "you know these walls are pretty thin. From my work bench out there, I can't help hearing what's said in here."

Debbie smiled at him. Bless him, it didn't make any

difference if he'd heard what they said. George had always been her best friend, advisor, money-lender, and champion-for-Debbie's rights in any differences she had with her father.

"What is it, George?" she asked.

He wiped his bald spot with the oily rag. "Well, bad as I hate to say it, I believe Milt Carver, Don's dad, has started all this ruckus over the lease to get *you* out of the picture."

Debbie felt her heart lurch. "Me? Why, what do you mean?" Something pricked her eyes.

"About ten days ago Milt stopped me downtown. It was in front of the *Journal* building, and he started askin' questions about you. Sure acted biggety."

"What did he want to know?"

George hesitated, fumbling for a match. "That's just it. I don't think he really wanted to know anything. He figures Don is getting too serious about you, and he was trying to give me a word-to-the-wise business." The old man puffed at his pipe angrily. "I should have bent his nose—hintin' to me that you weren't good enough for his boy."

Debbie felt as if her throat were closing. She turned back to the ledger in stunned quiet. So that was why Don was so careful never to say a word about how he

felt about her. . . . But she knew. She knew he liked
her a lot. She had seen it in his eyes. She had felt it
when they'd been together. But she had to say something to George, so she wet her lips and tried to make
her voice sound natural. "But surely, George, Mr.
Carver wouldn't try to break our lease over a personal—"

But George broke in, "Guess you don't know Milt
Carver," he snorted. "He's colder'n an ice worm."

"But Don and I aren't engaged or anything like
that!" Debbie was trying to figure this all out in her
own mind as well as explain it to George. "We have
another year in high school, and then he's going to
the Air Force Academy for four years! It's just ridiculous." Debbie's eyes stung at the unfairness of it all.

" 'Course it is. But nobody can tell Milt anything."
George knocked his pipe bowl against the palm of
his hand. "Milt's probably the richest man in Twin
Lakes, yet the men who work in his plant say the
Journal equipment is held together with bailing wire!"

"Just the same, it's not fair." Debbie protested.
"Even if he doesn't like me, it isn't fair to strike at
Dad and you."

"Don't you worry about your dad and me, Miss
Debbie. Anyway, I just sent off a letter that *might* put

a stop to Milt's game."

"Letter?"

He nodded. "The Aircraft Mechanics Association picks a 'flight operator of the year' every summer, and I sent in your dad's name. The other day the committee wrote that your dad is one of the finalists."

Debbie gulped. That was wonderful. "Why, George, do you honestly think he might win?" Wouldn't that be something?"

"Well, I was checkin' on his horoscope, and the planets are pretty favorable for him right now."

Debbie put her hand over her mouth to hide a grin, and nodded. George had been studying astrology for weeks. He was forever exploring unusual ideas. Before astrology, it had been Zen-Buddhism (whatever that was).

"When will we know who the winner is, George?"

"Couple of weeks, I guess. They asked me to send more details. The only thing is, I—" he ducked his head guiltily—"kinda mentioned the teen-age daughter Ben had taught to fly, and I guess I might have said something about a home-made sailplane, and how you might set a record in it. I figured that would cinch it for Ben."

Debbie swung around and hugged him. "Wowee! A

record!" Of course it was fantastic. Who ever heard
of a teen-age girl making a record in a homemade
glider? Still, it was something to think about. "You
know you could do it, if you tried, Miss Debbie."

Debbie shook her head, feeling as if she'd suddenly
been plopped to earth from an air pocket. But George
was looking at her hopefully; she had to say something. "But, George," she began, "one must have
special sealed instruments, official observers, and I
don't know what all."

"An official flight, even if it's just close to a record,
would help your dad so much," George said eagerly.

The vision of fame dwindled and Debbie felt guilty.
The important thing was to do whatever she could to
save her father's business, so she wet her lips and said
quietly, "Okay, George, if you think it will help, I'll
try. I'll try my very best."

George beamed happily. "We'll not say anything to
Ben. Let's surprise him. And I'll stay tonight and give
your glider a coat of wax. Might add half a degree to
its glide angle."

Debbie gave him a quick smile. "All right. But
don't forget, keeping a sailplane in the air depends
mostly upon finding the proper weather conditions."

"Don't I know it?" He winked. "That's what I'm

bettin' on—your weather savvy."

Debbie made weather antennae with her fingers, holding them beside her eyes. "It's due to my personal radar!" she laughed.

A record. Well maybe she could do something to make Don's dad think she was pretty clever, after all. *Not good enough for Don, indeed!* Again anger boiled up inside her as she quickened her step toward the apartment back of the office.

CHAPTER II

Don was a few minutes early for his flying lesson. At the window, Debbie watched him as he parked his parents' pink Cadillac. Then her breath quickened. Here he came striding to the office. She loved the way he walked, with the effortless tread of the natural athlete. Her heart was keeping step with his long strides. She could hardly keep from running to meet him, to match his tallness against her five feet, one and a half inches.

She drew in a long breath, thinking how handsome he was. She loved his changeable blue eyes, that were sometimes warm and quick, and sometimes cloudy and unfathomable. No wonder, if his dad had been giving him the works about going with her.

Something touched her heart as she remembered what George had told her, but only for a moment. Don had his father's determined jaw and dark hair. That jaw might mean he would stand up for his rights to go with anyone he pleased.

By the time he had swung open the door, her heart

had rushed up into her eyes and looked out. She had to pretend to be busy at the desk as he called out, "Hi, Deb! Got a fresh rubber band in the cub? Ol' Don's ready to aviate."

She whirled around and tried to put surprise in her voice. "Why, Don, is it time for your lesson?"

"Yep." He blew her a kiss and sat on the leather couch, idly flipping the pages of a flying magazine. His nonchalance wore a thin place in the tight string that had been holding her together for the last hour. She had to think of something to say quickly or she'd start bawling.

"I want to thank you again for last night," she said, and could hear the crack in her voice.

He ran the heel of his hand along one eyebrow. It was an unconscious gesture Debbie had noticed many times before. "It was only a movie and a malt," he said depreciatingly. "But we did have fun. Only trouble, eleven o'clock's too early to go home. Wish your dad wasn't so strict about that."

Debbie shrugged. Her father did seem a bit old-fashioned at times. "We can always come back here, and I can bring my record player in the hangar. Dad wouldn't mind that." Debbie had just thought of the plan. What fun it would be to sit on the couch and listen to dreamy soft music! But what was Don saying?

"That would be fine with me, except I've got orders from the top of the Carver household: 'Don't loaf around the airport.' "

His words brought back that little sticker in her heart. Her mouth felt shaky, but she could pretend as well as the next one. So she answered him quite casually, "Oh, your father doesn't object to your learning to fly, does he, Don?"

Don put down the magazine and shrugged. "He doesn't object, but he isn't exactly for it, either. I tried to tap him for the dough, but no go." He grinned up at her. "Mom's on my side, though. I explained that learning to fly would give me a big advantage at the Academy, and she's always sort of dreamed of me going there."

"I guess your father would rather you worked on the paper," Debbie said, feeling him out.

"He expects me to, later. But he's kind of sold on the Academy now, because it's supposed to be tough."

"I'll bet it is, too."

Don puckered his lips disparagingly. "It's a university with uniforms," he said. "Ol' Don can cut it."

For a brief minute Debbie felt a twinge of irritation. That was the one thing about Don that clashed with her own character. He was forever supremely confident. And it was even harder for her to bear because the confidence always seemed justified! Without appearing to half-try, his brilliant ball-carrying had sparked the Twin Lakes high school football team to an unprecedented state championship last fall.

His school marks kept his name among the top ten in his class, though he never seemed to study. Nor was it necessary for him to put forth an obvious effort to make friends. He had dozens of friends among the boys at school. And girls—well, more than a few passed Debbie and Don in the halls every day, ignoring Debbie, and following Don with their eyes, the way a cocker spaniel does when he's hoping for a pat on the head.

"Say, Deb, you're not planning to move, are you?" His voice broke off suddenly, and he looked straight into her eyes.

"Move?" she gulped. She stood there shaking her head for "no" like a dodo bird.

"Well," he sighed and grinned, "that eases the strain on the brain."

"Yes," she said, trying to hold her mouth still from its silly jerking. "It isn't good to change instructors."

"Aw, c'mon Deb, you know what I mean." There it was in his voice, in his look.

She turned back and smiled. "I hope so." She paused for a second and then asked, "What made you ask if I expected to move, Don?"

"I don't know. Something Dad said, I suppose. You know he's kind of hard to understand at times."

"I've never met him, but you must be very proud of him." Debbie was surprised at how she could keep the scorn out of her voice.

"Sure."

"And your mother, too. I think she is the most beautiful lady in Twin Lakes."

"Mom's my pal," he said, his voice suddenly warm.

Debbie waited, thinking he might continue, but he didn't. She promised herself that she'd not hint again for an invitation to the Carver home. After all, she'd known Don for seven months and they'd been going steady for several weeks. He certainly knew that he should formally introduce her to his parents. However, if the Carvers were really opposed to her, the only hope she had was in meeting them and attempting to change their minds about her.

She checked the green bow on her pony tail. "My glider is finished. I flew it this afternoon." She tried to keep the pride out of her voice. After all, he had to sell his jalopy to take flying lessons. He didn't have anything to have fun in. He had to borrow his dad's car.

"Yeah." He smiled. "I saw it as I drove up. Sure looks neat. I get a feeling, looking at the sailplane, the way it sits crouched and quiet and eager—I'd sure love to fly it after I solo in the Cub. Could I?"

Wonderful. She had wanted him to like it and understand how she felt about it. "Of course, Don, if you think it would be all right with your parents." She hadn't intended to say it. It had just slipped out unbidden.

He was silent for a moment. At last he said, "Are you sure you're not thinking of moving away, Deb?"

She hesitated. "The city council wants Father to liven things up out here before they renew the lease. But it'll work out. We're staying right here." She wished she felt as confident as her voice sounded.

"Oh, well, that's easy. Put on some air shows—parachute jumps, areobatics—stuff like that."

Debbie shook her head. "Father says thrill shows hurt flying, rather than help it."

The office door opened and Debbie's dad looked in. "Pardon me, but I am waiting, Don."

Don leaped to his feet. "Sorry, Mr. Mills. See you later, Deb."

Within a couple of minutes, Debbie heard the Cub speed down the runway. From its sound, she measured its take-off run; knew when the bright yellow wings slipped the earth's restraining bonds, then nodded subconscious agreement as the engine's song dropped an octave to climb speed.

She lifted half a dozen invoices, copying and extending them into the ledger from the adding machine; then, feeling the July heat return behind the rain, switched on the electric fan, hurriedly pinning down loose papers with old engine parts.

As the Cub's engine beat grew in volume, she made a quick check of herself in the little mirror she kept in her desk drawer. Was her nose shiny? Had the rain made her pony tail too fuzzy? Satisfied, she gave her reflection a knowing wink and went outside to meet Don and her dad.

She quaked inwardly at Don's landing approach. It was a bit high and much too fast. He was well down-field before he finally touched down, though the Cub's fat tires brushed the concrete as lightly as blown leaves.

Don spied Debbie as he taxied toward the hangar.

He took his hand from the throttle to wave. Debbie started to return the wave when her arm froze and her breath caught in her throat. Don was swinging the plane's wingtip perilously close to the hangar!

Debbie knew her dad had ridden with too many students ever to be lulled into relaxing his vigil. But he was allowing this student to bring the wingtip within a couple of feet of the building. Debbie's heart almost stopped. Then the dual throttle was closed, and the plane braked to safety. Thank heavens her dad had been there.

Don slid to the ground behind his instructor with no trace of his usual smile, "Guess I made a slight goof, Mr. Mills." Don evidently intended this to be an apology.

"Yes," Debbie's dad agreed soberly. "And this points up a thing I've been telling you. You must think ahead of an airplane. You're flying it until it's in the hangar, Don."

"All right, Mr. Mills." Don grinned, then looked at Debbie. "Guess I almost made your J-three-Cub into a J-two-and-a-half."

"You made a smooth landing just the same," she said in his defense.

"I'll buy you a malt, just for that." He was as

assured and cocky as ever. Nevertheless her heart warmed at his invitation.

"Shouldn't you return your parents' car?"

"Maybe your dad will let you have your car, and I'll meet you at Pearson's."

Debbie looked at her father. "I'm not allowed to drive the car alone," she said.

"I forgot," Don said. He shook his head in mock puzzlement. "The space age amazes ol' Don sometimes. You can buzz around the country in a flying machine, but aren't allowed to guide an automobile down the road." He turned his grin on Mr. Mills to show that he meant no offense.

"I'll admit," Debbie's dad said, "air travel isn't completely without danger. But it should be as soon as safe transportation to and from the airport is devised."

Don grinned, then ran the heel of his hand along his left eyebrow and made no reply. Perhaps he had just recalled why Debbie's dad was so afraid for her to drive the car; perhaps it had just occurred to him why she had no mother.

"If you want to collect that malt, Debbie—" her dad turned to her—"I'll drive you into town and pick you up later."

"Righto." Don saluted and left, still grinning.

"Okay, Dad," she said, hearing her voice rise to a squeak.

"What's the matter, Deb?" He came toward her.

"She's in love, and about time," George said, pushing through the door. "Girls always act this way when they're in love."

Her dad whistled softly.

"Oh, leave me alone, you two." She brushed past them. "I'll go fix my face, Dad."

She went to her room and shut the door. Standing there in front of her mirror, she whispered hoarsely, "Does it show *that* much?" Angrily she wiped lipstick from her mouth with a tissue. Then she shucked out of her jeans and slipped a blue summer cotton over her shoulders, letting the full skirt swirl about her slender legs. She jerked the green bow off her pony tail and brushed the shoulder length bob into a page boy.

She remade her mouth very carefully, dusted powder across her nose and looked again into the mirror, this time deep into the misty eyes of a feminine female. A smile lifted the corners of her mouth as she leaned forward, giving the girl in the mirror a big wink as she said, "Keep hold of the controls, Deb!"

CHAPTER III

It was after six that evening when Debbie's father retrieved her from Pearson's Drugstore. There, in the cool intimacy of a private booth, she had her moment to find out Don's real feelings for her, but she had somehow muffed it. She had the feeling that Don was holding back because of his father. Maybe a promise he'd made or something, but she didn't have time to think about it now. It was almost dinner time.

George was to eat with them, for he planned to wax Debbie's glider. She hurried around and prepared ground beef patties and fried potatoes, because both men preferred simple food. She diced a banana and a couple of marshmallows into a bowl of canned fruit salad, and topped this with whipped cream for dessert.

They had barely finished eating when the hospital called. An emergency case—a man with a brain injury

—had to be flown to St. Louis immediately. This was more or less routine. Ninety percent of all charter flights were emergencies of one kind or another. Debbie quickly stacked the dishes in the sink and followed the men outside.

They had rolled the TriPacer, three-nine-delta, from the hangar. George was removing the co-pilot's seat to make room for the stretcher.

"Did you get the weather report for me, Deb?" her dad inquired.

She shook her head. "The airway radio report isn't due for ten minutes yet. Shall I phone for it?" She was eager to help all she could.

"No. I'll pick it up en route. Case of this kind, I've got to go anyway." He turned to George. "George, you don't mind staying out here until I get back, do you?"

" 'Course not," George grinned. "I've sat with Miss Debbie many a time."

Debbie's father smiled. "She no longer needs a baby sitter, but I don't want her alone out here after dark." His glance covered Debbie like a warm caress. Old fuddy-duddy, bless him. At least she had grown up enough to not have a baby sitter, and that was something.

Far down the highway, the panicky wail of a siren

warned of the ambulance's approach. Debbie's dad got into the plane and fastened his seat belt.

A couple of minutes later a police car swung onto the apron, leading a white ambulance. While the ambulance made a quick turn and backed toward three-nine-delta, one of the policemen sprang from the patrol car and pushed ahead into the cabin. "Ben, the doc says this fellow hasn't more than three hours to get to the specialist in St. Louis!"

Debbie watched her dad's mouth slim out into a firm straight line. "Well, it's three hundred and seventy air miles, Travis, but I can average a hundred and twenty-five unless I get a bad break in the weather."

"His wife and kids are in the hospital here," the policeman said. "Wrecked their car out north of town a while ago."

Debbie saw her father's calm grey eyes suddenly narrow. "I give you my word," he said quietly, "I'll get him there within three hours."

Debbie caught a glimpse of a still white face as the stretcher was lifted into the TriPacer. A nurse clambored in after, followed by the portable oxygen equipment and several bottles of plasma.

Then the green and white plane taxied rapidly to

the runway and took off into the evening sky. The patrol car and ambulance left. Debbie clutched George's arm, and they walked slowly back to the hangar.

The hangar seemed empty with the three-nine-delta gone, though Debbie's glider was there, lightly poised on one wingtip, with the single wheel protruding through the bottom of the fuselage. Next to it sat the Cub. The Cub's air scoops were like big eyes, she thought, perpetually amazed at finding a propeller on its nose. The red Fairchild, six-eight-bravo, was parked behind in its shadow.

All this belonged to them—all these beautiful, wonderful birds of flight—and nights like this she knew that the three-nine-delta was doing the community a service that nothing else could. It might be the difference between life and death. Her eyes misted over.

George was rummaging about the work bench. "I notice the United States soaring team is lookin' for a girl pilot to represent the U.S. in the women's division," he drawled.

Debbie reached into the cabinet for the wax and some clean rags. "Do you mean for the international contests in Europe next spring?"

"Yep. All expenses paid, too."

"That's dream stuff, George. I suspect that you could be a tiny bit prejudiced. Besides, I haven't even earned my Silver-C badge in gliding."

George slammed a drawer shut and opened another. "That'll be easy for you," he said. "All you got to do is gain thirty-three hundred feet of altitude, go thirty-one miles, and stay up five hours."

"Sure," Debbie shrugged, "that's all!"

George ignored her sarcasm. "Maybe you could take me along, Miss Debbie, and try to break the record for flight with passenger! I know where I can borrow a sealed barograph to make it official."

Now she was paying attention. He might be making sense. "I didn't know there was a separate record for one and two-place flights."

"I think there is." He gave up his search of the work bench and turned, exhaling noisily. "Do you know where that wax is?"

"I have it, George." She grinned, holding it out to him.

"Humph! Why didn't you say so?"

"Now don't get grouchy or I won't let you help me." She smiled, cocking her head at him, and his pique vanished.

Two and a half hours later, they had finished all

but the rudder and fin. Debbie sat down atop one of the Cub's wheels, took a deep breath and licked the perspiration from her upper lip.

"I'll finish this, Miss Debbie. I know you're tired."

"I keep thinking how good that shower will feel, George."

"You go and take it. This is about done."

She accepted his offer with a smile. She had never felt more tired or dirtier.

When she returned to the hangar, she glanced at her watch. It was five minutes before ten. She brought two tall glasses tinkling with ice cubes.

"Lemonade?" She offered George a glass.

"Looks good," George said, trying a sip.

Then, while they were sipping the lemonade, the flash of automobile headlights swept across the hangar's open doorway. Debbie and George turned, watching as the car approached from the highway.

Seconds later, the Carvers' pink Cadillac pulled onto the apron and stopped. But it hadn't brought Don. It was his father who got out of the car and strode toward them. Of all people to see her hair in rollers, it would have to be Mr. Carver!

"Good evening," he said curtly, nodding unsmilingly at each of them. Then, addressing George, he came straight to the point. "Where's Ben Mills? I want to charter a plane at once."

Debbie caught George's twinkle of satisfaction as he nodded in her direction, indicating that she was the one to deal with in the absence of her father. "I'm sorry, sir," she said respectfully, "but my father is away on an emergency charter now. We don't expect him back before one or two in the morning; perhaps later."

Mr. Carver scowled as though she'd deliberately planned things this way. His heavy face grew redder and he spoke slowly, emphasizing each word. "Miss Mills, there has been a mechanical break-down in the press room of the *Journal*. The morning edition must go to press not later than three a.m. I must have parts here from Oklahoma City before that time." His tone suggested that that should settle the matter.

"We'll do whatever we can to help, Mr. Carver," Debbie replied quietly. "I'll call Wichita and try to locate a charter pilot for you." She went into the office with the two men following.

Ten minutes and five long distance calls later, however, the problem remained. Two wives reported husbands out on charter, two did not answer, and the last was preparing to leave, already booked.

Debbie pushed the phone to one side and sat in deep thought for a moment. At last she said, "There's a Central Airlines flight from Oklahoma City which comes through Wichita a little after three. If you could get your parts on board and meet it at Wichita, then you could drive back to Twin Lakes by four-thirty—"

"I thought of that an hour ago, young lady," Carver interrupted sharply. "What I can't seem to make clear is, the *Journal* must go to press at three, not five! Over nine thousand subscribers in this country expect it on their front doorsteps before six o'clock!"

Debbie could see that George was becoming angry. She sent him a warning look, then replied patiently to Mr. Carver, "I told you, sir, that we'd do whatever we could to help. There is only one other thing I know to try. If I can reach my father through the Airway Radio System, and if he will give his permission, I'll take a plane and go after your parts." She didn't feel in the least afraid. She was really anxious to go, but she wouldn't meet George's eyes.

For a second or two Mr. Carver looked at her with a mixture of suspicion and hope. Then he shrugged. "Go ahead." His manner implied that he expected little or nothing.

Debbie, her heart racing in excitement, reached for the phone and called Wichita Municipal Airport. She stated her request briefly. She asked that her father's reply be sent back via the low frequency weather channel, because this would allow her to hear his answer on the little radio in the office.

The fliers' world is a big-hearted one. Wichita agreed to relay her message to St. Louis radio. Debbie's dad should be almost there, if he had not already landed. She was informed that she could expect an answer within five or six minutes.

Those minutes were tense. No one said anything. Mr. Carver paced the floor. George drummed his fingers on the arm of the leather couch and hummed tunelessly. Debbie flicked on the low frequency receiver. It was the only radio equipment Twin Lakes Airport could boast. Its sole purpose, until now, had been to receive the twice-hourly weathercasts.

After a minute or two of background static, caused by the thunderheads forming in the west, the set came to life. "Twin Lakes Airport, this is St. Louis Airport. Take no chances, Deb." Debbie caught her breath as her dad's voice broke. But it went on, "If weather marginal, answer is negative. Repeat, negative. If you go, take George. Report hospital patient holding own. I'll return daylight. Rain here. St. Louis repeating special to Twin Lakes. . . ."

They listened as the relayed message was repeated; then Debbie switched off the set and turned to George. "You heard what he said, George. You must go with me."

"I'd ride with you any place, Miss Debbie."

Debbie bit her lips and smiled her thanks. She picked up the phone again and placed a call to Oklahoma City's downtown airpark.

In addition to the usual pilot's request for wind, ceiling and visibility, she asked for the barometric tendency and cloud sequence during the past six hours, this latter information being the stuff of which forecasts are made. The man at the other end of the wire supplied the data, and she nodded to herself, scribbling figures on the desk pad. Then she thanked her informant and replaced the receiver in its cradle.

After a quick call to the hospital, passing on the welcome news about the man's condition that her dad had asked her to do, she faced Mr. Carver again. "If you will call and arrange to have your parts at the downtown airpark in Oklahoma City," she said, "George and I will leave at once."

Mr. Carver avoided her eyes. His gaze traveled from the radio on her desk to her worn flats. "Very well, Miss Mills," he said, and there might have been the faintest hint of apology in his voice.

Debbie and George went into the hangar, closing the office door behind them. "It's clear and unlimited at Oklahoma City, George," she said. "There's a small low-pressure area in between, at the eighteen-thousand-foot level, which may cause some cloudiness, but I wouldn't call that 'marginal.'"

George wagged his head wisely. "What about those thunderheads over in the west?"

"They're local. Probably be gone by the time we get back." George chuckled. "You know this is a thing I never knew to fail. Do a wrong to somebody, and it won't be long before you need that somebody real bad. 'Course if I'd been you, I'd probably have told Milt Carver to go feather his prop."

"You'd have done no such thing," Debbie chided. "He needs help."

"Well, anyhow, if he'd bought some decent machinery, he wouldn't be in this pickle." George leaned into a wing strut of the Cub, rolling it aside and clearing a path through which they could move the Fairchild.

While George checked the six-eight-bravo, Debbie returned to the office for the final word from Don's father.

The parts would be waiting, he assured her, his voice crisp and businesslike once more, and he would wait right there until she got back.

"If you'd like to go with us, Mr. Carver," she said, "I'll lock up here." She crossed the office and turned on the runway lights.

He glanced through the west window to the western horizon, where lightning flashed from a line of thunderheads. "No, thank you, Miss Mills," he said firmly.

Debbie spread an air chart on the desk and studied it for several minutes. She drew a careful line on the map, measured its length and angle with her plotter ruler, then made some pencilled notations on the map's margin.

She looked at her watch and turned back to Mr. Carver. "It's ten twenty-nine now. I estimate Twin Lakes return at one forty-seven a.m." She spoke with confidence. "It's a hundred and eighty-one air miles each way. We could do better except for a cross wind, but you'll still have plenty of time—"

"The plane's ready, Miss Debbie," George called.

"Coming, George!" Her heart sang as she climbed in and fastened her seat belt. Maybe she *was* an *air-hawk*, as Don had once called her. In the air she felt at home, light, free as the air itself. She loved every minute of flying.

Minutes later, she leveled off at four thousand feet. She carefully trimmed the plane, then tuned the radio. George stared into the night, apparently watching the faint blue reflection of the exhaust on the underside of the wing.

Debbie was glad he was along, because night flight could be lonely. Far above the surface, life seemed to have disappeared with the sun, and the world was huge and dark and quiet. The lights winking here and there in the blackness were cold, mechanical things, and were no proof at all that people were down there.

Debbie put on her headset and called Air Route Traffic Control at Wichita to give her flight plan. This approved, she tuned the L. F. receiver and waited for the familiar "dah-dit, dah-dit" radio signal which marked the north Airway Green Four. She would follow Green Four to its intersection with Airway Blue Five, then ride Blue Five to Oklahoma City.

A couple of minutes later, the radio signal surged loud and clear in her earphones as she intercepted the invisible air highway. Debbie continued into the airway until the "dah-dit" blurred into a steady hum, then turned on course. She was now in the center of the beam. If she strayed left, a "dah-dit, dah-dit" would predominate; to the right, the "dah-dit" would return. A newer, high frequency radio system, called VOR, was much better and easier to follow, but the equipment was expensive and Debbie's dad had not installed it in their planes yet. Debbie turned down the volume and relaxed against her pillow.

Off the right wing, a new quarter-moon hung above the horizon's dark rim. Filmy bits of cumulus swept by beneath, their tops faintly silvered with moon-glow. Stars were sharp and clear—the cold and intense blue-white ones, and the familiar orange ones, such as Antares, in the heart of Scorpius.

Forty-five minutes outbound from Twin Lakes, they passed over a chrome thread in the darkness below. It was the Salt Fork of the Arkansas River, and they were right on time. She had selected it as a check point. She called Ponca City Radio, reporting her position. She would have liked to have talked a little, but the voice from out of the night sounded bored— or maybe he was only sleepy. She signed off, "Fairchild, six-eight-bravo, out."

They were halfway to their destination now, and through the propeller's blur a portion of the sky ahead had begun to glow, as though lit by the flame of a tremendous bonfire below the earth's edge. They flew directly toward it, as a buzzing insect courses a distant yard light.

Half an hour later, this crown of radiance on the world's rim had spread, crept close, and revealed its source—countless points of light arranged in neat rows on the surface—the eyes of a city, blinking sleepily from the prairie night. Debbie closed the throttle and wound the stabilizer crank to the normal glide position. The clock in the instrument panel held its hands close together. It was eleven-forty-five p.m.

She entered the downtown airpark's traffic pattern at eight hundred feet, pivoted sharply with her left wing pointing down at the North Canadian River bordering the field, then coasted onto the runway. Exultation filled her heart. She had made the first lap . . . and the return would be easy. She heard George chuckle.

"Sure set 'er down like she was full of eggs, Miss Debbie." It was the first time he'd said a word since take-off.

Debbie, pleased at his words, gave him a wide smile,

braked sparingly and turned off the runway onto the taxi strip.

Mr. Carver's parts were waiting. George loaded them into the baggage compartment and stayed with the plane to oversee its refueling, while Debbie went to the airport café for a glass of milk. She gulped the milk hurriedly, feeling ill at ease all alone so late at night. As soon as she had drained the glass she fled the café, after gathering surprised looks from the counter man and a couple of pilot customers. Plainly they were unaccustomed to seeing an unescorted teen-age girl, with her hair in rollers and minus make-up, on the field after midnight. Feeling slightly wicked, Debbie returned to the flight line. She did wish she'd remembered to put on a little lipstick.

Five minutes later, she and George were airborne again. They climbed out over the southern part of the city, circled back over Bethany, and took up their homeward heading of one-zero-one degrees. Wheatland Radio's high-pitched hum, marking Blue Five, was steady and reassuring.

At cruising altitude, Debbie leaned the gas mixture, trimmed the plane to fly itself, and sank back with an eye on the instrument panel. It was not necessary for her to read each gauge individually. If any needle

strayed the width of a kitten's whisker, a warning
would flash in her mind. George tipped back his head
and promptly went to sleep. A lot of company *he* was.

Before Debbie knew it, they were there. Debbie
guided the six-eight-bravo down between the double
row of lights marking Twin Lakes' runway. The thunderheads had passed over, leaving the concrete wet and
shiny, the air clear and cool. She could see Mr. Carver
waiting in the splash of light outside the office doorway. She wakened George. "We can't be there," he
exclaimed.

Debbie swung onto the apron and cut the switch.
She saw Don's father refer to his watch as she slid
to the ground behind George. Her watch showed one-
forty-five a.m. It was a minute ahead of her estimate.

George carried the box of parts inside. "Here you
are, Milt," he said quietly.

Mr. Carver nodded soberly, extracting his check
book from his pocket. "How much do I owe you,
Miss Mills?" His voice was smooth, but Debbie
thought she caught a little note of respect in it, and
a quick smile came to her lips.

"I can't accept pay, Mr. Carver. F.F.A. regulations
forbid persons under eighteen to fly commercially."

His eyes narrowed suspiciously. "I don't care about

that. I didn't come here asking a favor. It is my policy to pay for what I get."

Debbie bit her lip. "I'm sorry." Oh, why did he have to be so patronizing, so hateful? She swallowed hard and tried to speak casually. "But I can't violate the law. And I'm sure my father would agree."

"You'd rather have me obligated to you. Is that it?" His voice was almost insulting now.

Debbie grabbed George's arm as he started to open his mouth angrily. She certainly didn't want any more black marks against her account than Mr. Carver already imagined. The calmness of her voice surprised her. "No, Mr. Carver." Her lips were trembling again. "It was a service to the community, as you said. The people expect their papers at six."

Mr. Carver reached to the floor for his box of parts. "I'll settle with your father," he said darkly, then strode through the door, slamming it behind him.

"Of all the ill-mannered, ungrateful, patronizing stuffed shirts I ever saw—he's a cockpit full of them," George said. "Didn't even thank us. Thinks his money can repay any favor or kindness—the big lug." George was still muttering to himself as Debbie went on back to the apartment and fell on the bed to sob herself to sleep.

CHAPTER IV

Debbie was still asleep when her father rapped on her bedroom door the next morning. She opened one eye and checked the clock beside her bed. Nine-fifteen!

"Just a minute, Dad!" she said, slipping into her robe as she went to the door, grinning to herself. She'd never even undressed last night!

"Sorry I overslept." She gave him a quick kiss. "When did you get back? Have you had your breakfast?"

He held her shoulders with both hands and shook her lovingly. "In order mentioned, I'd say oversleeping is okay. . . . Got here an hour ago, and yes, I've eaten, thank you."

"Smarty." She yawned.

He caught her to him in a spontaneous hug. "I was mighty proud of my big girl last night." Then he gave her a playful shove. "Hurry and get dressed," he said. "There's someone here to see you."

Debbie was suddenly awake. "Who?" she whispered. Maybe Don had come to make amends for his dad's bad manners.

"A lady." He lifted his eyebrows.

"Who, Father?"

"Mrs. Milton Carver."

Debbie quaked inside. Now what?

She raced to her closet. "Be there in a minute," she called over her shoulder.

Slipping out of her wrinkled clothes, she chose a green polished cotton dress to wear.

A few minutes later, Debbie entered the office and her dad presented her to Don's mother. Mrs. Carver smiled. Oh, she was beautiful! And her voice was silken as she held out a hand to Debbie. "I'm so happy to meet you at last, Deborah!" She was a replica of the most high fashioned model in *Vogue;* poised, slender, and looking much too young to have a son Don's age.

"If you will excuse me," Debbie's father said, "I have a student waiting."

"By all means, Mr. Mills," Don's mother said. "I shouldn't want to interfere with your appointments."

As the door closed behind her father, Debbie said, "Won't you sit down, Mrs. Carver? May I bring you some tea?" She couldn't keep the lilt out of her voice. This gracious lady was here to thank her for helping them out with the parts last night.

Don's mother sat on the leather couch. "Nothing, thank you, dear. And I do want to apologize for popping in like this without warning." An emerald-cut diamond flashed as she smoothed her expensive linen dress. Her hair was almost the color of Debbie's, except for an unusual orange cast. Debbie wondered what its natural color would be. Probably a light brown, considering Mrs. Carver's gray-green eyes and delicate complexion.

"I'm happy you came, Mrs. Carver. I've admired you for a long time." Debbie could hear the warmth in her own voice—she meant what she said.

Mrs. Carver seemed pleased. "Thank you, Deborah. I, too, hold you in high regard. In addition, I am quite grateful, as is Mr. Carver, for your timely assistance to the *Journal* last evening."

"It was my pleasure to be able to help." Debbie tried to make her language as correct as Mrs. Carver's. She had never noticed how worn the leather couch was until she saw Mrs. Milton Carver on it.

Don's mother hesitated, her expression growing serious. "Mr. Carver was so concerned last night. He simply *lives* for that paper, you know. And talking with him this morning, I discovered that he is quite upset because you wouldn't accept pay for your service."

Debbie explained why she couldn't lawfully take money for the flight, adding, "I'm sure I owe Mr. Carver an apology. I should have told him of the situation before take-off. I'm truly sorry, Mrs. Carver, that this oversight on my part has caused him to feel badly." She hugged her elbows to her sides. She sounded like a character stepping out of one of Dickens' novels.

Don's mother smiled again. "I think that you and I can put things right." She opened her purse, a small glazed straw affair, and took out a check. She placed it on a pile of ragged flying magazines on the table before her. "I want you to have this, Deborah, as a *gift* from me to you." Her voice held the satisfaction of one who had just solved a very difficult problem. Debbie's eyes blurred for a minute in hurt.

The office swivel chair creaked as Debbie bent forward. The check was made out to her in the amount of one hundred and twenty-five dollars, exactly the price of a charter trip to Oklahoma City and return. Debbie's throat seemed to close over. She shook her head and finally got the words out: "It is extremely generous of you, Mrs. Carver," she said slowly, praying that she could keep the tears out of her voice, "but I can't possibly accept it. I would feel that I'd evaded the law in some way."

"But, my dear, this is not for your trip to Oklahoma City. It is a personal gift from me to you!"

Debbie couldn't say a word. She only shook her head.

Mrs. Carver wouldn't give up, though. "Please don't make up your mind just now, Deborah. Put this aside somewhere, and consider further. You *must* allow Mr. Carver and me to express our appreciation of a very brave and courageous girl."

Debbie blinked back her tears. "Very well, I'll show it to my father. At the very least he will be grateful for your offer. Certainly you have made it clear why Don is so proud of you and Mr. Carver."

Mrs. Carver flicked a careful look at her. "My son is—at any rate I like to think he is—a cut above average." Whatever warmth there had been in Mrs. Carver's voice was gone now. "Of course, like all youngsters, his thinking tends to be somewhat immature at times." She paused, lightly smoothing her left eyebrow with the heel of her hand—a gesture Debbie recognized immediately.

"Mr. Carver and I are determined that he shall have every opportunity to achieve a happy, useful future. We want him to finish his education and finally choose a wife possessing a similar educational background." As she finished, Don's mother looked at Debbie with what might have been hostility for the space of a heartbeat, then smiled as if to say, "We do understand each other, don't we?"

Debbie bit her lip, trying her best not to show her hurt. She kept her lips smiling as she said, "I'm sure that you'll never have cause to be disappointed in Don." It seemed inane, but she couldn't think very clearly.

"I'm sure of it," Mrs. Carver said, getting to her feet. "Parents who live up to their responsibilities are much less likely to be disappointed." Her smile was warm again as she offered her hand to Debbie. "I have enjoyed talking with you, Deborah, and *do* keep the check, dear!" And then she was gone. The door closed behind her, with only the faint scent of subtle perfume lingering to mark her tension-filled visit.

For a long moment Debbie remained standing,

trance-like, in the center of the office. Now that Don's mother had gone, it was hard to believe that she'd actually been there and said the things that she had. The sound of the car departing outside seemed to release the tension. Like a jointed doll, Debbie walked stiffly to the window and looked for the Cub. It was high in the west. A student was learning stall recovery.

Debbie turned back into the office. Maybe her heart would start beating again. But just now she felt like a sleepwalker.

She shook herself. She had to come out of this trance. She went out into the hangar. George was at the far end, tapping on something with a hammer. Debbie ducked beneath the tail of three-nine-delta and went to join him. She needed to share her hurt. "What you making, George?" she asked, going over to him.

"Just straightening out the dents in this piece of fairing. Might need it sometime." He held up the sheet of curved aluminum, inspecting it critically. "Clara gone?"

"Clara?"

"Clara Watson—married to Milt Carver."

"Did you know her before?"

"The Watson place was right next to ours. Only

about twenty miles from here. I remember Clara when she was in pigtails. Of course she was still a little girl when I left home."

It seemed incredible to Debbie. "She was reared on a farm?"

George turned indignantly. "Lots of people were reared on farms. I was. Can't see what's wrong—"

Debbie hastened to correct the impression she had left with George. "Oh, George, I didn't mean it that way. I practically was, too. An airport, a mile and a half from town, isn't much different. I only meant—well, you know."

"Clara comes from a good family," he said, searching for his pipe. "They were hard-working, God-fearing people. Saved their money. Her dad built the first grain elevator in Twin Lakes. He was a wealthy man when he died." George poked tobacco into his pipe and waved it at her. "Let's go inside so I can light this, Miss Debbie."

They threaded their way between the Fairchild and Debbie's glider; passing the TriPacer, George stopped abruptly.

"Just a minute." He bent beneath its nose, studying the under side of the fuselage between the landing gear struts.

Debbie bent down and watched George as he wiped a few specks from the shiny green surface. "It's probably some oil that has blown back from the rocker covers," she said.

"Oil belongs *in* an airplane, not *on* it," he replied. He stuffed his pipe back into his coveralls and began unfastening the cowl snaps. "I'd better pull those rocker covers and put in new gaskets."

"It surely is easy to see why none of our planes has ever had an engine failure," she said.

"Airplanes are like people," George said. "They'll treat you like you treat them."

"Most people, you mean."

"Clara get uppity with you?"

She told George about the check.

He nodded as she finished. "About as I expected. Here, help me lift this off." He went to the other side of the plane and pushed the cowl across to her. "Hold it!" George ducked back under the nose, and together they lowered the engine cowl to the floor.

"George, I don't know what to do to change her mind about me! How do you convince such a person? She acted as if I were a stink-bug or something." Even telling somebody about it made her eyes sting with unshed tears.

"Miss Debbie, you never know what goes on in other people's minds. I expect part of it is that Milt and Clara are scared of Don running off and getting married." George went to the work bench, returning with his tool box and a handful of clean rags. He carefully wiped number one cylinder-head, and then leaned close to it, peering through his horn-rimmed glasses.

"Hand me a three-eighths box end out of there." He motioned to the tool box.

Debbie passed him the wrench. "Don wouldn't do that, and neither would I. I've seen a couple of teen-age marriages at school. They moved in with their parents. Besides, Don wants to go to the Airforce Academy more than anything. He pretends that it's nothing special, but I know him. It's the most important thing in the world to him. And I also want to go to college." Debbie went on, trying to swallow the persistent lump in her throat, "I must have an education so I can research in weather, George."

"I know all that, Miss Debbie," George replied softly. "I'm just sayin' that's one of the things the Carvers are probably worried about. There's bound to be other things, too. Now hand me that feeler gauge so I can check this valve entrance."

Debbie pushed the tool box close to George so that he could reach things for himself. "More than anything, I've hoped that Don's parents would like me and—" She halted, realizing that she was dangerously close to tears, and that would never do. Besides, what was the use of moaning all over the place? She intended to make the Carvers like her.

"You know, I think Mr. Carver would be nice, once you came to know him."

"You sure got an imagination," George said dryly.

"I mean it. I've been reading his editorials in the *Journal* every morning. I think he's a sincere person."

George shrugged. "Maybe. He's hard to figure. I've been wondering if some of the trouble wasn't that Milt resents your dad's war record. You was too young to remember, Miss Debbie, but Ben came home a pretty big hero. Milt was turned down for service, I guess."

"He couldn't help that!"

"Of course not. But it's tough on he-men like Milt to be classed 4-F. He's the kind that would rather go over there and die than have folks think he lacked courage."

Debbie was silent as George went to the wall cabinet for new gaskets. When he came back she said, "If Dad was a hero, why doesn't he ever want to talk about the war? Is it because it was so horrible?"

"You know your dad, Miss Debbie. He's sort of sensitive, and he left a lot of good friends out there. Also, he didn't much like the publicity. I remember one day in San Diego—this was right after the battle of Midway—he told some reporters that they had the wrong guy. He said, 'I didn't get nearly as close to that enemy carrier as some of the other pilots in the squadron. If you want to write a story, write about them—they won't be coming back.' Then your dad just walked away."

Something pricked at Debbie's heart. "You and Dad were on the *Enterprise* together. Was the *Enterprise* in the battle of Midway?"

"She sure was, Miss Debbie," George said proudly.

George turned from his task to squint into the distance. "Well, it was June, 1942, more than two years before you were born. In fact, it was before Ben met your mother. You know he came home for thirty days right after Midway, and that was when he met Judith. She was working in a little book store on Coronado Street in San Diego." Debbie wanted him to hurry. She never got enough of his stories about her father and that dainty, lovable girl, Judith, who had been her mother. George swallowed, then continued:

"Well, as I was saying, at that time most of the Navy was at the bottom of Pearl Harbor. Then, at Midway, the Japanese fleet moved in to finish off what was left." George extracted his pipe. He stared at it for a moment, apparently without seeing it, then returned it to his pocket. "We had thirty-seven SBD's on the *Enterprise* and sister carrier. You know what a SBD was?"

"Yes," Debbie answered in a breathless whisper. "That was the Douglass Dauntless dive bomber that Dad flew in the war."

George nodded. "Like I said, we had thirty-seven of 'em. They were old pre-war crates and some of 'em had already been shot up, but it was all we had then. Well, Admiral Spruance, our commander, he sent them thirty-seven SBD's out to stop the enemy fleet!" George raised his chin and stood very straight. "It was the most stupid and the most magnificent thing I ever saw. Think of it—thirty-seven old beat-up SBD's against a whole task force—including three enemy carriers!"

George whipped out his soiled bandanna and blew his nose noisily. Stuffing it back into his coveralls, he concluded quietly, "When it was over, two enemy carriers were on the bottom and everything else was on the run. Our pilots caught 'em next day, and got the third carrier. It was the turning point of the war in the Pacific."

Debbie stood enthralled. She took in a long, exhilarating breath. "It makes a person proud to be an American, doesn't it?"

George turned back to the three-nine-delta's naked engine. "Ought to. All during the battle those boys would come back to the ship, planes all shot up, get gas and more bombs, and go right out again. When Ben brought his plane in it was so full of holes it wasn't nothing much more than a loose formation of rivets. Had to junk it. Wasn't worth fixing."

"Really?" Debbie said, her eyes blurry. Her dad had really been a hero—just too modest ever to talk about it, she supposed.

"You don't need to let on to your dad that I told you about it," George said. "But you might want to remember it next time Clara looks down her nose at you."

Debbie was quiet for a long time. It might seem strange, but she couldn't find it in her heart to try to hurt or get back at Don's mother, and most certainly she'd never bring this story up if it shamed them.

CHAPTER V

Debbie went back to the office to post students' flight times, enter the day's receipts and make up the bank deposit. This done, she posted the invoices left over from yesterday, then sorted the mail which her dad had brought from the post office earlier. There was a letter from Shayna Todd, Debbie's cousin, who planned to spend a week with Debbie this summer.

Shayna said she'd arrive at the Wichita airport at noon on August second. Well, in spite of Shayna's odd personality, it would be nice to have another teen-age girl around for company. Debbie's local girl friends, especially Sammie Goodman, sometimes came out to the airport to visit, but they never stayed long. And Debbie didn't get to town often, except to school. That was because she wasn't allowed to take the car. If her dad just wouldn't be so stubborn about that, she could have a lot better time when Shayna came.

Debbie typed a reply to Shayna's letter and splurged an airmail stamp on it. That would make it seem more urgent, and cause Shayna to feel that Debbie was anxious to see her.

Debbie put the letter with the bank deposit back so that her dad could mail it when he went to town, then crossed the office to check the barometer. Her own observations, added to the regular airway forecasts, confirmed that this would be a good soaring day.

Turning back to the apartment, she busied herself making sandwiches and salad for lunch.

At eleven-thirty she served the lunch on trays in the hangar. The hangar was the coolest place, with the big doors open at each end. Whatever breeze there was found its way through.

Debbie's dad lifted the napkin covering the plate of sandwiches. "Which ones have peanut butter, Deb?"

"None," she said, pouring the iced tea. "You've been eating too much of it. I don't want you to get fat like other men your age."

He grinned at her and selected a ham and cheese. "Looks as if it'd be a good day for gliding. Want me to give you a tow after we eat?"

"I hoped you would. I'm going to try to go to

Wichita and back."

Her dad's sandwich stopped halfway to his mouth. "It's forty air miles to Wichita, Deb, an eighty-mile round trip! If you run out of up-currents, you can't get out and push, you know; you'll have to land. Why not stay within range of the airport?"

Debbie sent a quick glance at George. He was munching a sandwich innocently. "Well," she said, "for one thing, I would kind of like to qualify for a 'Silver-C' badge."

Her father continued with his sandwich, chewing thoughtfully. He sipped some iced tea, then said, "It's all right, I suppose, as long as you make sure that you have enough altitude to get from airport to airport. I certainly don't want you down in a pasture somewhere with no way home."

"Oh, no, I won't—that is, I'll be careful." Debbie broke off as a car swung from the highway and came crunching over the gravel connecting the road to the apron. It was Sammie Goodman in her parents' Rambler.

"Hi, Sammie." Debbie walked out to meet her, glad as always to see her.

Sammie got out of her car. "Hi, Debbie." She waved to George and Debbie's dad. She was small, about Debbie's size, and dark. She wore her hair page boy fashion, with bangs, and reminded Debbie of a Mayan princess. Her true name was Samantha, but even her parents called her Sammie.

Sammie's parents had moved to Twin Lakes just before Christmas, and she and Debbie had become friends almost from the first. Sammie's father worked on the *Journal*.

"You're just in time for lunch," Debbie said. "Come in and help yourself."

"No, thanks." Sammie laughed. "I just ran out for a second to tell you that I'm having a slumber party Saturday night to christen our new house. I'm asking you and Marge and Saralee."

"Sounds swell, Sammie."

"Well, don't forget. Come any time after seven."

"Thanks, I'll be there. Do you have time to come in and see my sailplane? It's all finished."

"I'd love to, Debbie, just so I get home before twelve o'clock."

They went into the hangar, and Sammie ran her hand along the glider's smooth and shiny wings. "It's just beautiful, Debbie." Then her expression became puzzled. "Debbie, I'm terribly dense, I suppose, but I simply can't comprehend how a glider can stay in the air for *hours* without an engine to hold it up."

Debbie laughed. "You're not alone. I've talked to airplane pilots who didn't understand that very well, Sammie. What you do is find up-currents of air to gain altitude. You see a sailplane always glides downward through the air. However when it flies within air that is rising faster than the sailplane is sinking, then it is sort of like—well, imagine how it would be for a man to try and descend one of those ladders that fire trucks use—you know, the kind that keeps stretching upward to get to the top of a tall building. As long as the ladder is going up faster than the man is coming down, he won't reach the ground."

"Do you mean there's a lot of air going straight up all the time?"

Debbie shook her head. "No, on lots of days there isn't any at all. But on warm sunny days, especially in summer time, different spots on the ground absorb or reflect the sun's rays differently. Over the warmer places, the air gets heated and starts to rise. These warm up-drafts are called 'thermals,' and to a glider pilot, they are stones across a pond; as long as he can hop from one to another, he won't sink to the bottom."

"Aren't they invisible?"

"Sure. But you know what sort of places on the ground will make them. A wheat field, for example. And the top of a thermal 'most always turns into a little cumulus cloud, because the moisture in the rising air finally condenses in the cool upper sky."

Sammie seemed doubtful. "It surely looks like a chancy thing to me," she said.

"It isn't hard." Debbie smiled. "Sailplanes don't weigh much, and their long wings produce lots of lift."

"Just the same," Sam laughed, "I think I'll stick to airliners. The more motors the better." She turned to leave and said, "I was going to ask you and Don to play tennis with Larry and me this afternoon. But Larry, the dope, told Kay Winthrop we'd come to her house and play on Kay's private court. I knew you wouldn't go there."

Debbie took a grip on herself and said calmly, "I don't have anything against Kay."

Sammie was unimpressed. "Don't tell me you like the way she throws herself at Don."

Debbie felt the hot blood come into her cheeks, but she raised her chin and said, "I've really never noticed."

Sammie grinned. "See you later." And she ran out

to her car.

"G'bye, Sammie. Thanks for the invitation."

Debbie turned and went back inside, stinging at the thought that Kay Winthrop would be playing tennis with her Don that afternoon. Don was the dope. Couldn't he see what Kay was trying to do?

All the time that she was changing from her dress to her jeans, she was seething inside. The poor stupe would buy her a malt, too, feeling that he'd be obliged to. Oh, well, the sooner she could dust off such thoughts in the clear cool upper air, the quicker she could forget Kay and her obvious designs on Don.

Dressed for fun, Debbie stood beside her glider, near the downward end of the runway, waiting for her dad to bring the Cub and tow her into the air. She had uncoiled the nylon line, and it stretched three hundred and fifty feet along the edge of the airstrip.

Over on the apron, George was hanging up the gas hose, and her father was climbing into the refueled Cub. A minute later, he taxied by, grinned at her, then continued down the runway toward the opposite end of the towline. Debbie reached inside the cockpit, testing the tow release, then attached the line beneath the nose and climbed into the glider.

CHAPTER VI

At one-twenty-nine p.m. Debbie passed near the Wichita Municipal Airport. Her altimeter registered forty-seven hundred feet, and she could not enter the controlled airspace over the city without radio clearance. She swung southward, feeling for thermals above the green pastureland. A two-way radio in the glider would be handy, but would add weight—and expense.

The time of decision was at hand. Thunderheads were building up between Wichita and Twin Lakes. Should she gamble that she could remain aloft until they moved beyond her home field, or should she take no chances and turn back now? A round trip of eighty miles was a very respectable accomplishment in a motorless plane (though far short of the two hundred one mile record) and she was virtually assured of making her home field if she started back now.

However, there were hours of daylight remaining, and she had an exceptionally good start if she dared try for a truly great flight. "I don't know why I'm arguing with myself," Debbie said aloud to the wavering altimeter. "I promised George that I'd do my best!" She pressed the left rudder and followed the highway toward Winfield. A moderate thermal reversed the altimeter's downward course.

Debbie wondered if other glider pilots were always as reluctant as she to leave the security of an airport. Cross-country soaring was made up of one crisis after another. All landings were forced landings. Therefore it surely was comforting to have an airstrip within gliding range. But gliders had some advantages: They could fly as slowly as thirty-five miles per hour, and required but a fraction of the landing space needed by airplanes.

Twenty minutes after leaving Wichita, Debbie was below two thousand feet and becoming a bit anxious about an up-draft when a cumulus forming ahead offered another reprieve. She was too low to take a chance on missing the thermal, so she searched the ground for the warm spot that had spawned it. There —that sandy hillside bordering the highway. She noticed the cars because, at that height, they had grown considerably in size. They reminded her of mechanical mice, scooting along minus their tails.

Coasting toward the hill, Debbie watched one of the "mice" that seemed to be wound up tighter than the others. He was pulling away at a high rate of speed. "You'd better slow down for that curve, mister." She spoke aloud again.

Then, a second later, Debbie stared in horror as the car swung wide entering the turn and disappeared in an explosion of dust at the roadside! She pivoted on a wing, thermal forgotten, and unconsciously whispered a prayer for the occupants of the wrecked auto below.

Slowly the dust blew away and she could see the car, lying on its side a hundred feet or more from the road. It had leaped the ditch and come to rest beyond a clump of bushes.

Debbie continued to circle tightly above, unmindful of her dwindling altitude. Had anyone else seen the accident? She watched two cars approach the curve, both traveling in the same direction. She could see none coming from the other direction. The first car entered the turn and continued around the hill without slowing. The second followed. Neither was aware of the wreck hidden from view by the clump of foliage!

Debbie did not hesitate. She pushed the stick forward and recklessly threw away her precious altitude. She did not think of her mother, at least not consciously; her mind held but a single thought: she must get down there and stop the next passerby. There had been no movement from the smashed car, and Debbie knew that, at that very minute, someone's life could be ebbing away for lack of help.

A choice of landing places was no problem. There was no place except the highway itself. She established her final approach carefully. She must touch down and stop north of the hill, because her wings would reach several feet on either side of the road. A car was coming from the opposite direction now, but she would be down before he reached the scene.

There was a bit of a cross-wind to complicate matters, but she held one wing slightly low and kept a small bit of rudder to that side. Fifty feet now—twenty—ten—Debbie opened the air brakes on top of the wings, destroying the remainder of her lift. The single wheel absorbed the gentle bump, and she pulled the wheel-brake lever with all her might.

The glider's tail rose high, and the sleek craft

skidded fifteen or twenty feet on the steel runner below its nose, coming to a halt squarely in the center
of the roadway. Debbie scrambled out just as squealing
tires signaled the arrival of the car she'd seen approaching a minute before. A man jumped from the
car and came running to meet her. "Are you in trouble, miss?"

Debbie wasted no words, "Do you have first-aid
training?" She ran past him toward the curve. "Hurry!
There's a wreck down here!"

The stranger recovered quickly. "Where?"

Debbie pointed and continued running.

"Wait!" the man called. "You stay up here and
send the next car for an ambulance! I'll go do what
I can!" He plunged into the ditch and through the
bushes.

Debbie looked back up the road. Some cars were
coming. They'd be forced to stop, because her glider
blocked the highway. She was waiting as the first of
them came to a stop. It contained a man, wife, and
two children. Debbie told them that there'd been an
accident and that an ambulance was urgently needed.

"We passed a service station about a mile back,"
the wife recalled. "We can telephone from there."

"Notify the highway patrol, too!" Debbie called as

they turned around and drove away.

During the next ten minutes, the highway—which had seem sparsely traveled shortly before—was suddenly full of cars. A dozen or more were held up from each direction, with more arriving every minute. Debbie enlisted the help of three drivers and, with the aid of a borrowed wrench, unbolted the left wing of her glider.

This allowed traffic to move once more. There was room for only one car at a time to go by, but by taking turns, with Debbie directing, they soon cleared the jam.

Meanwhile, a highway patrolman had arrived. He ran to the wreck with his first-aid kit, then returned a few minutes later to relieve Debbie of her traffic-control duty.

Debbie retreated to stand by the cockpit of her craft.

At last the ambulance came. It waited on the curve while several men stumbled across the ditch with two stretchers; then its doors slammed and it was gone, its siren fading mournfully in the distance.

The patrolman took down Debbie's story. When she'd finished he asked, "How are you going to get your glider out of here, Miss Mills?"

"If only I had a tow rope, you could pull me into

the air behind the patrol car—that is, if you don't mind."

"How much rope do you need?"

"For a car tow, I need about eight hundred feet."

The patrolman whistled. "Know where you can get it?"

Debbie nodded. "If I can get to a phone, I can call my dad at Twin Lakes Airport, and he can bring one."

"That's fine," the patrolman said, "because regulations make it impossible for me to use the patrol car for that. But you don't need a phone," he added, smiling. He took the radio microphone from the patrol car and called his headquarters. He explained Debbie's need, directing that it be relayed to the Twin Lakes Police Department who, in turn, would call her father. He then made his report of the accident, concluding with word that he would remain at the scene until the glider was airborne again.

It was a long wait; an hour and five minutes, according to Debbie's watch. And every minute that passed increased the thunderhead build-up in the direction of home. Finally the sound of an auto horn, far down the highway, claimed her attention.

The car was coming fast, and it looked like—why, it *was* the Carvers' Cadillac! It was Don! She ran to

meet him as he screeched to a stop behind her glider.
"Don! Whatever are you doing here?" Bless him,
she'd never needed him more.

He got out, grinning. "Well, you needed some help,
so ol' Don made with the horsepower." He went to
the rear of the car, tugged the coiled towline from the
trunk and, dragging it back, addressed the patrolman
in a good-humored drawl. "We'll fling a rope on that
critter, Sheriff—" he motioned to the glider—"and
drag 'er back to the ranch."

"Okay, stranger," the officer replied. "But y'all
watch your speed goin' back. I shore would hate to
have to dry-gulch the feller who rode to the rescue."

Don laughed, and Debbie broke in impatiently,
"Why didn't Dad come, Don?"

"He'd just taken off with a student when the police
called. There's no radio in the Cub, and no way to
get word to him, so George sent me."

"Do your parents know you came? They'll be having conniptions!"

"Deb, I didn't have time to go through channels."

"I surely do appreciate it," she said. "I hope it's
all right with your father and mother."

Don hesitated, sobering. "For you, Deb, I'd have
tucked that rope under one arm and run all the way

if necessary," he said quietly.

Debbie took his hands and tried to thank him with her eyes. She wanted to fling her arms about his neck. It was one of the nicest things he'd ever said to her, but with a dozen passing strangers staring at them, she could not offer more concrete evidence of her feelings.

The highway patrolman solicited the aid of two motorists and, arming them each with a flare, sent them in either direction to halt traffic. The sailplane's wing was reattached, the silver craft swung around, and the towline secured to the rear bumper of the Carver sedan. Debbie climbed into the cockpit and fastened her seat belt and shoulder harness. "Fifty miles per hour is fast enough, Don."

The patrolman looked anxiously down the highway. "Are you sure that you can do this safely, Miss Mills?"

"Hey, Officer," Don said, "Deb could fly a hangar door off the ground in less room than this!" He started his engine and drove slowly down the road, uncoiling the line.

The officer got into the patrol car and waved to Debbie. "Good luck!" he called. "And thanks for a fine job!" He then sped off to lead the way for Don during the glider's launching.

A few minutes later the towline grew taut; the glider began to roll and, as Don accelerated, the narrow wings grasped for support in the warm air. Within seconds, Debbie was off the road and climbing steeply.

At five hundred feet she could see that Don and his escort were nearing the roadblock. She dropped the line and turned back toward the hill. Maybe the thermal was still there. It was—but, this close to the surface, it had little momentum. The variometer showed but two hundred feet per minute ascent. Perhaps it would grow stronger higher up.

Thirty-five minutes and several mediocre up-drafts were required for Debbie's glider to struggle to four thousand feet. It was after four o'clock, and the thermals were not as plentiful as they had been earlier. The best part of an unusually good soaring day had been lost because of the accident.

From that altitude, Debbie could no longer recognize the Carver car, but she knew that Don was following. He'd not go ahead until he was certain that she could make it to Twin Lakes. Bless him. Debbie was not at all sure that she could.

Then, as Wichita Airport inched by, a few miles off her left wing, she realized that she could not trail the storm clouds into her home airport. Twenty-five miles or so to the northeast Debbie could see dark streaks beneath the thunderheads: rain. The rain would kill the thermals, and by the time the sky cleared, the sun would be angled too low in the west to make new ones.

If it had not been for Don down there, she'd have turned southeast, circled around the storm and attempted to slip home ahead of it; but Debbie knew that he would try to follow, and there was nothing except primitive farm roads that way. She continued above the highway, looking ahead for a suitable landing place. She'd go as far as possible.

Ten minutes later Debbie ran out of altitude. From three hundred feet, she lined up on a fenced pasture about a quarter mile from the highway and coasted over a narrow farm road to a soft landing. She opened the canopy and slipped to the ground. The foot-high grass was wet, the ground beneath soggy.

She trudged back to the fence and climbed through to the muddy road just as Don swung off the highway. With an alarming amount of slipping and splashing, he drove up and stopped. "Hi, lady! Out of gas?"

Debbie sighed and waded through the mud to the car. "I'm out of *everything*—" she got in, then smiled at him "—except someone to look after me when I get into trouble."

"It's a pleasure." He grinned. "What next?"

"We'd better go. We're only about twenty miles from home, and you should get the car back. Dad and George and I can come after the glider. Probably have to take off the wings and tow it home on the ground."

"Okay." Don swung to the left side of the road, stopped, wound the steering wheel, then shifted to reverse. The back wheels spun ineffectually. He began working the gear selector from *drive* to *reverse*, gunning the engine with each change of gear. This set the car rocking; then suddenly the wheels found traction and the heavy sedan shot backward into the muddy ditch behind.

For a brief instant Don's face mirrored bewilderment and gathering anger. His expression clearly said, "This car can't do this to Don Carver!" He jerked the gear selector into *low*. "Deb, you slip over here and give it gas. I'll push."

"Don't you think we should walk to the highway and try to get—"

"No," he interrupted grimly, "I'm getting it out of here if I have to take it out piece at a time!" He burst out of the door, slamming it behind him, and sprawled in the mud.

Debbie was beside him in a second. "Oh, Don! Don!" she wailed. She had no handkerchief, and gently wiped his face with her hands, transferring the mud to her dress. "You're not—I mean—are you all right?"

Don sat for a moment, making no attempt to get up. Outwardly, his anger was gone and his blue eyes held only a wounded, defiant look of hurt pride.

"I moved the car just as you stepped out," Debbie said. "I can't tell you how sorry I am!" She put her face against his forehead. Sometimes a white lie is justified, she thought.

He stood up, pulling her up with him, and smiled. "That's okay, Deb." He lifted his arms to put them about her, then stopped, looking down at the mud and water dripping from him. He laughed. "Guess we'd better get the car out."

Her heart was doing a little dance again. He'd almost kissed her—almost put his arms about her. He'd come racing after her in the pink Cadillac. Oh, la-de-da, that stand-offish sweet thing *did* love her, after all. Who cared if he wanted to play a few tiresome tennis games with Kay?

CHAPTER VII

It was raining when Debbie and Don arrived at
Twin Lakes Airport. It was almost six p.m. Nevertheless, they had been fortunate because, defeated in
their efforts to free the car from the mud, they had
started out on foot to seek help when a farmer with
a pick-up truck happened by and cheerfully pulled
the Cadillac from the ditch.

Debbie hadn't worried about anything. Her glider
was okay. The Cadillac was a ball of mud, but that
would be easy to clean, once she and Don got at it.
She was grateful that her glider was on this same
farmer's land, a thing he seemed pleased about instead
of angry. He offered to keep an "eye on it" until she
returned. Sitting close to Don as they rode home, her
heart was warmed and filled with something akin to
contentment. People didn't have to tell you if they

loved you. They just showed it, as Don had today, racing after her when she needed him.

As they drove onto the rain-shiny apron, Debbie's dad and George were waiting in the hangar doorway. Anxiety lined both their faces, and that stabbed Debbie's heart.

Don continued inside the building so that Debbie could get out without getting wet, as if either one of them could be further harmed by a bit of water.

Debbie's father was clearly concerned. He opened the door for her. "I was getting a little worried—" He saw the mud on their clothes. "Great Scott, Deb! You didn't wreck your glider, did you?"

Debbie grinned, shook her head and started to explain, but as soon as her father determined that she was all right, he interrupted, "Mr. and Mrs. Carver are waiting in the office." Then he turned to Don. "George called your parents as you asked, but they've been pretty upset, so I went after them. I'm afraid they thought—well—" He didn't finish, but opened the door leading from the hangar into his office and waited for Debbie and Don to precede him inside.

Mr. and Mrs. Carver were sitting close together on the leather couch and staring at the doorway as Debbie followed Don into the office. Their faces were grim

and accusing. Debbie took a deep shuddering breath.
Now what?

"Hi," Don said weakly. "Er, I'm sorry I kept the
car so long. Deb was forced down again, and we got
stuck."

"I'm a dope," Debbie said, trying to force a smile
that she certainly didn't feel.

Clara Carver closed her eyes and pressed her eyebrow with the heel of her hand. Debbie felt sorry for
her, for she could see that Don's mother was very
close to tears. Mr. Carver's eyes did not waver.

"Your mother and I were afraid you'd had an accident," he said, getting to his feet.

"Deb needed help," Don said, and Debbie caught a
trace of defiance in his voice.

Mrs. Carver rose beside her husband. "Donald,"
she said almost prayerfully, "you went to help Deborah, and you became stuck in the mud—" she forced
a little laugh that seemed near hysteria— "and that's
simply *all* there is to tell. Isn't that right?"

Debbie bit back a stinging remark. Couldn't they
just take a ride, without Don's mother and dad trying to make a big deal out of it? But Don smiled at
his mother and said smoothly, "That's right, Mom.
I'm sorry that it caused you to worry. We came home

the minute we could get the car started." He went over and took her hand, and to his father he said, "I'll clean the mud off the car, Dad."

"All right, Son."

"Goodness, Donald, don't concern yourself about a little mud on the car." Mrs. Carver smiled. "Neither your father nor I is angry. When you didn't come home when we expected you to, we were afraid there'd been an accident. We hear about so many such things nowadays." She had regained her poise. *The unjust sentence had been commuted.* Debbie gritted her teeth. No, they hadn't eloped or anything like that!

Then she remembered her manners and stepped forward. "The whole thing was my fault," she said, "and I'm deeply sorry." But her father interrupted.

"I'm more to blame than either of the kids," he said, smiling. "I sanctioned Debbie's flight, and she's my responsibility." Then he gave Don a wide smile. "Your son's going to Debbie's aid certainly exceeds the small favor Debbie performed for the *Journal*. I'm very grateful to Don, and I know Debbie is."

Debbie knew her father well enough to understand that he was gently chiding the Carvers with this reminder. But Mr. Carver seized it eagerly. "Well, now, Don, that's fine. You know we Carvers like to stay square with the world."

"It's late," Don's mother said. "Thank you very much, Mr. Mills. Coming Don?"

"See you later, Deb," Don said, lifting an eyebrow as if there were some kind of intrigue afoot.

After they'd gone, Debbie related the day's events to her dad and George, then went to their apartment to shower and change from her bedraggled clothes.

The next morning Debbie returned her glider to the airport. She was able to fly it back as a result of her idea for a simple though unusual means of launching it. "Fishing poles—we can move it with fishing poles," she said.

"Fishing poles?" Her dad grinned. "What kind of bait shall we use?"

"Okay, Mr. Smarty, I'm serious. Listen: Attach the towline to the glider and uncoil it. Then, downfield, make a thing like a fotball goalpost with the poles. Stretch the end of the line between them for its crossbar and—"

"Ah ha! Now I get it! The fishing poles will hold the line up in the air while I fly over and snag it with the Cub!"

Debbie nodded.

"That should work," he agreed thoughtfully. "The

army used to do it that way. But you realize that, despite the considerable resiliency in nylon rope, you'll still get a pretty good shock when I engage the tow-line."

"It won't be nearly as great as a catapult launch from a carrier," Debbie pointed out.

"Well, no, but just the same, you buckle your shoulder harness tightly and keep your head against the headrest."

"I'll keep my eyes shut, too," Debbie teased.

"You do that," her dad said dryly. "Come on, George. Run me back to the airport; then you come back here and hold the glider's wings level for the air launch."

An hour later, Debbie's dad made a long low approach to the pasture. There was a short length of line, terminated with a big metal hook, trailing below the Cub's tail. Debbie watched it sail by a few feet over her head, and head unerringly for the towline stretched between the fishing poles three hundred feet away. She saw the two lines merge and prepared for the shock to follow, but it came with a suddenness that she had not anticipated. Between heartbeats, her silver bird leaped twenty feet into the air. Debbie leveled off a bit, caught her breath and looked out to the left wingtip, half expecting to see George still holding on there. He wasn't, of course.

Later, with the glider safely back home, and George suspiciously inspecting it for any sign of damage, Debbie fixed a salad and sandwiches for lunch. She served them as usual on the work bench in the hangar.

The old mechanic lifted one corner of his sandwich, checked its contents, then settled atop one of the Cub's wheels. "You folks seen the mornin' papers?"

Debbie shook her head, her mouth full of lettuce and tomato.

"I glanced at the *Journal*," her dad said.

"The *Wichita Sun* has a piece about Miss Debbie helpin' those men in that car wreck," said George.

Debbie's eyes widened, but the mouthful of salad kept her quiet.

"There wasn't anything in the *Journal* about it," her father said.

"Humph," George grunted. "Didn't expect Milt Carver to print it."

Debbie gulped her food. "Do you have the Wichita paper, George?"

He nodded. "Just now had time to look at it." He tugged a folded newspaper from his coveralls and handed it to her. "That patrolman said some nice things about you."

Debbie read it with growing pride and excitement. The reporter made much of the fact that she had flown a motorless plane more than sixty miles. He stressed, too, that Debbie was but seventeen, and that she might have saved the life of the more seriously injured of the two men. She passed the paper to her dad. *"Golly, I'm sort of a celebrity,"* she whispered, enchanted.

"So's Yogi Bear," he said.

She bit her lip in disappointment. She glanced at George, but the old man had turned his head. "I suppose it is sort of exaggerated, isn't it?" she asked tentatively.

"No," her father said, "it looks like a good, straight piece of reporting. The danger of exaggeration is *here.*" He tapped her head. "Understand, Deb, I'm proud of you and of the way you acted, but heroines are for T.V."

She gazed through the hangar doorway into the distance. "Just the same, I think it would be nice to be famous."

Her father shrugged. "Fame's all right—as a by-product. It's pretty worthless in itself."

"Well, you have to *be* somebody to get famous, don't you?"

"That's not my point. I'm merely trying to say that there are lots of true heroines in the world you'll never hear of. There are housewives, secretaries, schoolteachers, or dime-store clerks who meet life with more courage and honor than many of the famous!" The calm gray eyes focused to infinity, and he concluded, "It can require as much or even more courage simply to stick to one's job and make a living, to rear a child, to face squarely one's duties, than it does to perform the most widely heralded act of heroism. In other words, Deb, public acclaim is no sure test of greatness." He grinned and added, "End of speech."

Debbie smiled. "I can see the truth in that, all right. I only meant that it would be nice to be famous if somebody *deserved* to be famous."

Her father sighed. "And I only meant that none except the humble deserve to be!"

She laughed. "I won't worry about that! If I ever do get famous, you'll see to it that I don't get snooty!"

"I hope so," he replied, looking at her very strangely. It was as if he actually expected her to be well-known some day. And it gave Debbie an odd feeling; an exciting, heart-quickening lift, mixed with fright. Certainly she'd dreamed of being a celebrity—but she'd never truly believed that she would be.

They ate in silence for a time. Then George said, "Milt and Clara sure had their manifold pressure up last night, didn't they?"

"Yes," Debbie's dad agreed, "and it was mostly my fault. Next time Deb starts across country in her glider, I'm going to tag along in the Cub."

Debbie nodded vigorous agreement. "I don't want Don to bring his parents' car after me again. In fact, considering how they feel about me and all, I'm not going anywhere else in it—not even to a movie."

"This sounds like a roundabout way of bringing up the subject of your driving our car again."

"It would be nice if I were allowed to," she replied frankly, "and I'd be careful. But whether you change your mind about that or not, I'll not go in theirs again."

Her father considered this.

"All right," he said, "you can have our car next time Don asks you to go somewhere."

She smiled. "Thanks. That will solve one problem."

"Well, I told you I'd back your decisions in this."

"You know, Ben," George mused, "I been thinking. What we need for this lease thing is clear proof that the city council's charge isn't so."

"Yes," Debbie's dad conceded, "and in any other

business that would be easy. Trouble is, the average person doesn't know much about airplanes or running an airport. Do you realize that seven out of ten people in the United States have never flown?"

George frowned skeptically. "That's hard to believe, Ben. This's supposed to be the space age."

"Maybe so, but few schools have courses in aeronautics, and all that most people know about flying has been picked up from television or the newspapers. You know what that amounts to."

"Yeah," the old man said disparagingly. "Watched a T.V. pilot handling the controls last night; thought it was a fellow backing a truck into a phone booth."

Debbie's father laughed. "That's my point," he said. "A great deal of what people 'know' about flying isn't so. No wonder lots of people are still afraid of airplanes; they simply don't understand them."

"I don't see how it can be helped," said George.

"Perhaps it's not too important as far as the older people are concerned. The space age will belong to Debbie's generation."

Debbie cocked her head, squinting thoughtfully. Her dad's mention of the lack of air education in the schools, coupled with his concluding remarks, had sparked an idea. "Listen, everybody, why don't we start a free course in aeronautics? The council wants some activity out here, and we might get some new flight students from it! We can borrow chairs from the high school, and, Dad, you could give blackboard talks here in the hangar one night a week."

"Sounds like a good idea to me!" George said.

"For just anyone at all who wants to come?" Debbie's dad asked.

"Have it for junior high and high school students, but let older people come if they want to," Debbie suggested.

Her father hesitated. "Do you think the kids would come?"

"There's not much to do around Twin Lakes," Debbie pointed out. "They'll come the first time because they're curious. It's up to us to make it so much fun they'll want to keep coming."

"By golly, Deb, that's a challenge!" He turned to George, "Think you could interest young people in airplane engines?"

The old mechanic grinned. "Ben, you ever see a young fellow who wasn't interested in a smooth-runnin' engine?"

"We'll do it!" Debbie's dad whirled back to her eagerly, "And we'll make a special rate for rides over town, too!"

Debbie caught his excitement. "We'll call them 'flight-seeing trips,' and charge a penny a pound, and let the kids hold the controls a little!"

"You bet! And I'll go over to Wichita and borrow some movies from Cessna and Beech, and we can be host to a fly-in breakfast every month!"

"Roger!" Debbie agreed. "We'll put some *zing* into things out here!" She tossed her pony tail excitedly.

Her dad sobered. "You know," he said slowly, "there could be a speck of truth in the city council's charge. Maybe I haven't been doing all that I could have to promote flying out here. Instead of sitting around, blaming the high school for not teaching aviation, it's time I rolled up my sleeves and did something about it!"

"Let's make it our goal to reverse the statistics in our town," Debbie enthused, "so that we can say seven out of ten Twin Lakers *have* flown!"

"Roger!" her dad said.

CHAPTER VIII

After lunch, Debbie and her father drafted a two-column advertisement to be placed in the *Journal*. It was headed, "Free Aviation Movies," and the text was aimed principally at Twin Lakes' teen-agers. The shows were to begin on the coming Tuesday night.

"We don't want to use the words 'educational' or 'classes,' " her dad said, "because that might scare away some of the kids. I'll explain when they get here that we're frankly trying to foster interest in flying, but that we're all going to have as much fun as possible in the process." He then gave Debbie the keys to the car, suggesting that she take the ad downtown at once. "No need to waste any more time, Deb. Our lease runs out September first. I'll take three-nine-delta and go over to Wichita right now for the films."

"Okay." She started to leave, then turned back. "Is

it all right if I advance myself some money on my salary?"

"How much?"

"About ten dollars."

He frowned. "I don't like this 'advance' business, Deb. It reflects poor management. You get twenty a week for keeping the books—where in the world does it all go, anyway?"

"For the past two years most of it has gone into the red pig to pay for my glider—but you only raised my pay to twenty dollars last Christmas."

"Well, if it's for something you need, okay. But don't forget, it comes out of your check Saturday. I've never been able to understand why it takes so much more money for a woman than for a man."

"One reason is because you haven't had a new suit since I graduated from junior high."

"My blue suit is perfectly good yet."

"Sure; you only wear it to church. It's sort of dated, though."

"You're not ashamed of me, are you, Deb?"

"Don't be silly, Father. It's just that I want you to look like the successful man of the world that you are."

He pretended shock. "*I am?*" Then he grinned, adding, "Maybe I should buy a new yellow convertible, too."

"You should—but you won't."

"You're doggone right, I won't! The way business has been the past couple of years, I do well to put your college money aside every month!"

Debbie pretended to be properly impressed. But she *did* keep the books, and it seemed to her that they weren't as poor as her father's attitude suggested. "Maybe if we get a bunch of new customers, we could afford one," she said.

He shook his head in mock sadness. "Now I know why relief agencies are necessary; they're for poor, helpless men who have daughters!"

Debbie stuck out her tongue at him and flounced from the office.

Driving down Main Street, she spotted the Carver's plush sedan parked near Pearson's Drug Store. On impulse she swung into the curb beside it. Maybe Don was inside.

But as she dropped a nickel in the parking meter, she glanced up to see Don's mother emerging from the Vogue Shop next door. Mrs. Carver was accompanied by Mrs. Winthrop, whose husband was president of the First State Bank of Twin Lakes. Mrs. Winthrop smiled and nodded, although Mrs. Carver's expression did

not change when she saw Debbie. "Hello, Deborah."
That was all; cool as could be.

Debbie responded with a friendly "Hello" to each,
then continued toward the drugstore. She almost col-
lided with Kay Winthrop coming through the door.

"Hi, Debbie!" Kay thrust a tiny bottle at her,
"Smell." Kay was Debbie's age; blonde, pretty, and a
bit scatterbrained.

Debbie smelled dutifully. "It's exquisite, Kay. What
is it?"

"It's new. It's called *Escape*, and it's terribly exclu-
sive! See you. Mum and Clara are waiting for me!"

Debbie smiled a reply and entered the store.

It was cool inside, and quiet. It was the torpid quiet
of an empty drugstore on a hot summer afternoon, and
the lazy siesta atmosphere was disturbed only by the
air conditioner's drowsy hum. The booths in back,
which were teen-age territory, were unoccupied, and
the juke box dark. Mr. Tibbs, the pharmacist, sat at
the soda fountain sipping a coke. Mr. Pearson, having
just sold Kay the bottle of perfume, was behind the
cosmetics counter. They both spoke, calling Debbie
by name. In a town of fourteen thousand population,
there are few strangers.

Debbie took a fountain stool. "Could I have a cherry

coke, please, Mr. Pearson?"

"Sure, Debbie." Mr. Pearson was a small, thin man with a high-pitched voice. He seemed to take pleasure from the patronage of Twin Lakes' teen-agers. His own children were grown and married.

He came behind the soda fountain, put a scoop of ice in a glass, added a squirt of cherry syrup, then placed the glass beneath the coke dispenser. He stirred it vigorously and set it before her on the marble counter top. "There you are." He took Debbie's quarter and turned to the cash register.

"Would you give me the change in nickels, Mr. Pearson? I need them for parking meter money." Debbie didn't actually need the nickels, but it called attention to the fact that she had the car downtown alone.

He placed the nickels on the counter and tilted back his head to peer at her through his steel-rimmed glasses. "Quite a splash you made in the Wichita paper this morning."

"Yeah," Mr. Tibbs chimed in, "maybe Twin Lakes has another Amelia Earhart here."

Debbie was pleased but, for some strange reason, slightly embarrassed. What did real celebrities say when people praised them? "I just happened to be the only one who saw the accident. I didn't actually do very much."

Mr. Pearson nodded approval. "I like modest people," he said. "Just like your dad—folks'd never know some of the things he did if they waited for *him* to tell it."

"What I don't understand," Mr. Tibbs said, "is how you keep that thing up in the air without a motor."

"By using air currents, as a sailboat does," Debbie explained. "It's really just sky sailing."

"But what if you don't find the right kind of air currents?"

"Then you come down." She laughed.

"A glider isn't much good for anything, then—except for fun, I mean," Mr. Tibbs summed up.

"Well, I suppose not," Debbie said. How was it possible to explain the way it felt to have wings? How could one describe the wind's whispered fantasies tumbling over themselves in a mind enraptured by the beauty of shining cloud-canyons? What earth-bound person would believe that, in the high and lonely places, she could put out her hand and sense a Presence just beyond her fingertips?

"I always said I'd be willing to fly," Mr. Tibbs was saying, "so long as I could keep one foot on the ground."

Debbie forced a smile. She'd heard that corny expression a million times since she'd been old enough to understand English. She finished her drink and, slipping from the fountain stool, idled past the cosmetics counter. She paused to examine a vial of *Escape*. "How much is this, Mr. Pearson?"

The druggist did not move from behind the soda fountain.

"Twelve-fifty," he said, polishing his glasses. He knew very well that Debbie could not spend twelve dollars and a half for perfume.

She set it down carefully and pretended to consider. Then, tongue in cheek, she inquired, "Would you by any chance have a fifteen-cent cake of soap that smells like it?"

The two men were still chuckling as she went out.

A few minutes later, Debbie had submitted the ad to the *Journal*, specifying that it was to appear daily, in both the morning and evening editions of the *Journal*, through the coming Tuesday. She asked the cost, requested that a bill be sent, then, in sudden inspiration, said to the advertising manager, "This 'new look' at the airport might be good material for a feature story, don't you think?"

The advertising manager considered. "Yes, it might

be at that, Miss Mills. Of course, it's not in my department. Wait a minute and I'll check with Mr. Goodman—your ad will start in tonight's paper." He disappeared, and a few seconds later Sammie Goodman's father came from behind a glass partition.

"Hello, Debbie."

"Hi, Mr. Goodman."

"About your activities at the airport—what is it that your father proposes to do?"

Debbie told him of their plans, concluding with an explanation of the "fly-in breakfast" idea. "We'll invite all private pilots and their wives who live within two or three hundred miles. We'll serve hot cakes and bacon and eggs in the hangar, and then we'll have sort of a rally, like sports-car people have. You know, give little trophies for precision landings, maybe a handicap race to Wichita and back, things like that. It should bring twenty or thirty airplanes at least, and maybe as many as a hundred people to visit our town."

"I see," Mr. Goodman said. "It sounds pretty good. I'll see what I can work up on it. I'll give you a ring if I need more infor—" He broke off, looking past Debbie to nod respectfully. "Good afternoon, M.C."

Debbie turned, smiling, and added her "Hello" as Don's dad walked up to join them.

"Hello, Miss Mills. Will you pardon me?" He addressed Mr. Goodman. "Weren't there any calls or letters on yesterday's editorial, Paul?"

"No, sir."

Mr. Carver frowned. "We usually get *some* response. Why should yesterday be any different?"

Mr. Goodman shuffled his feet uneasily. "Frankly, M.C., I don't believe that yesterday's editorial was quite up to your usual standard."

Mr. Carver glared at the feature editor, and Debbie waited for the Carver wrath to break about Mr. Goodman's head. Debbie liked Mr. Goodman, and Sammie was Debbie's friend. "Yesterday's editorial *wasn't* as good as usual, Mr. Carver," she said. Then, realizing what she'd done, she held her breath, frightened and amazed at her audacity.

Mr. Carver slowly turned to impale her with the sort of look he might have bestowed upon a stink-bug squashed underfoot. "Did you read it, Miss Mills?"

"Yes, sir. I always read your column."

"Are you interested in world affairs, Miss Mills?" His tone made it clear that he did not believe her.

Debbie frowned and cocked her head. "Well, to tell the truth, not as much as I should be. I guess I'm interested in people."

"I fail to understand," he said sarcastically, "how a professed interest in people is gratified by reading my views on foreign aid or crop subsidies."

"It *is* sort of hard to explain," Debbie said. "Maybe it's because you make those things sound like people problems rather than world problems. But mostly, I like to read your column because you are never afraid to take a stand on anything. My father says that takes a lot of courage."

He stared at her for several long seconds. "Did Ben Mills say that?"

She nodded.

He hesitated again. He was obviously pleased, although he didn't want to show it. "Courage doesn't have anything to do with it," he said, much subdued. "It's my duty."

Debbie smiled up at him. "George, our mechanic, gets pretty angry sometimes at the way you criticize the Democrats."

Mr. Carver's hostility was completely gone now. "They deserve it!" He allowed himself a faint smile. "Those people are a menace to the country."

"My favorite," she said, "was the one you did about a month ago—the one about men wearing Bermuda shorts."

Don's dad chuckled in recollection. "Pretty good, wasn't it?"

"Wow-ee! I'll say!"

"It almost cost me the advertising account of Wayne's Men's Store, but it was worth it," he said proudly. He turned back to Mr. Goodman, "Sorry I interrupted, Paul. You and Debbie go ahead with whatever you were discussing." He smiled at them and walked away with a spring in his step.

Sammie's dad watched his boss's retreating back until Mr. Carver was beyond earshot. "If I had a hat on, Debbie, I'd sure take it off to you!" He grinned.

Debbie whirled around on her toes. Her first little victory with Don's dad. *Oh, my dear kind sir, I haven't even started yet!*

CHAPTER IX

Returning to the airport, Debbie was elated with her unexpected victory at the *Journal* Building. Mr. Carver had even called her "Debbie." Surely she had made a giant step toward winning his friendship. However, she mustn't get her hopes too high, because it seemed clearer than ever now that Don's mother was actually the "field general" in the campaign against Debbie. Nor was Clara Carver likely to respond to simple, human warmth as her husband had. Debbie, being a female herself, instinctively understood that a mother could ruthlessly thrust aside a normal sense of values during a battle for what she believed to be her child's best interest. This would be especially true of a strong-willed woman such as Mrs. Carver.

Debbie parked in the shade near the front steps of the apartment and walked around the hangar to the office. George had the cowling off the Fairchild, doing something to its engine.

Debbie cooled off before the office fan, then returned to the hangar to tell George of the headway she'd made with Mr. Carver.

But the old mechanic was skeptical. "Did he say why didn't he put in the paper what you did yesterday?"

Debbie shrugged. "Maybe there wasn't room, or maybe he just didn't consider it newsy enough."

"Humph! If you ask me, Milt's got a lot to learn about runnin' a newspaper. That story about you was news! Yesterday he left out the horoscope. Next thing you know, he'll stop the *Dear Abbey* column; then what have you got? Nothin', that's what!" George snorted indignantly and dug into his tool box.

Debbie hid a smile. "Mr. Goodman is writing a story about the movies and things we're going to have."

"Well, I hope Milt okays it—but I wouldn't bet on it."

"Don't be so pessimistic!" Debbie scolded.

"Aw, I'm sorry, Miss Debbie—it's just that I get so dad burned mad when somebody tries to push you around."

"Don't you worry, George," she replied positively.

"Like you said, everything's going to work out all right!"

Half an hour later, Debbie's dad eased three-nine-delta onto the runway. He had a planeload of movie film and other paraphernalia designed to tell people about airplanes. His friends in the public relations departments at Beech and Cessna had loaned him as much material as the green-and-white plane could carry. They had even furnished the movie projector.

While they were unloading, Debbie's dad said, "Mr. Robinson, over at the Cessna factory, told me something interesting this afternoon. He said that one of our bankers here, Bill Winthrop, is buying a new Cessna."

"Mr. Winthrop?" Debbie was incredulous.

"Why, he's never been off the ground, Ben!" George put in. "What would he do with an airplane?"

"I don't know," Debbie's dad said. "He told them to deliver it here next week."

"Maybe Kay is going to learn to fly," Debbie said. "She's his daughter." But even as she suggested this, Debbie knew that it couldn't be the answer; Kay just wasn't the type. At the controls of an airplane, Kay would be a threat to every plane in the sky—and to herself as well.

"Or maybe," George injected ominously, "Winthrop's gettin' ready to put someone in here as soon as we're kicked out."

"Now listen," Debbie's dad said, "we can think of all kinds of unpleasant possibilities if we try. It's possible that he intends to use it for bank business."

"So who's goin' to fly it?" George demanded.

"Maybe he's going to hire a pilot."

"I don't like your theory any better'n mine," said George.

Debbie's dad laughed. "Well, we'll wait and see. There's no point in worrying about it."

A minute later, Don arrived for his lesson. Debbie did not get to talk with him, except for an exchange of greetings, because it was exactly three o'clock, and her father liked to keep on schedule. As the Cub took to the air, Debbie went into the office to confront the day's book work. She accomplished little, however, for both Sammie and Marge Bennett called to talk about Debbie's adventure of the day before and the attendant publicity in the *Wichita Sun*.

July passed away—apparently of sunstroke—and on Monday Debbie postponed the launching of her sailplane for the fifth consecutive day. Each hot and humid afternoon produced a multitude of thermals,

but not the big ones, with high clouds forming, that she
needed for a serious record attempt.

She was more confident about trying for a record
now. The eighty miles or so that she had flown last
week served as proof to herself that she could keep her
glider airborne indefinitely if lifting air were present.
In addition, the two emergency landings—one on a
narrow highway, the other in a tiny alfalfa field—had
helped to dispel much of her apprehension about landing in improvised places.

Besides, if a record or near-record would help her
dad to be chosen "Flight Operator of the Year," it
would certainly be worth all the effort she could put
into it. If her dad received this honor, and there were
the free movies and fly-in breakfasts and all, the city
council would have no excuse to terminate the lease.

However, if the Carvers were determined to remove
Debbie from the scene, and if, as seemed likely, the
council followed Mr. Carver's wishes, then no amount
of increased activity at the airport would have any real
bearing on things. The only solution under such circumstances would be a change of heart on the part of
Don's parents. Nevertheless, Debbie was going to fight
on all fronts. She'd help her dad do everything possible to meet the city council's demands; and she'd

win the respect and friendship of the Carvers if it were humanly attainable!

It was three-thirty p.m. as she stood on the scorched apron, shielding her eyes from the sun, and watching the Cub overhead. Don was in his ninth hour of instruction, and Debbie suspected that this might be his day to solo. Her dad never divulged such news in advance, believing that it tended to make a student nervous.

Don had made three perfect landings in a row. Now he approached again, flared out his glide at exactly the proper time, and eased the Cub onto the strip. Its fat tires made a "chirrup" of protest as they brushed the concrete, and the little yellow plane rolled to a stop.

This time, however, Don did not gun the engine to go around again. His instructor evidently requested that he taxi to the hanger. There, Debbie's father slid to the ground. "You take 'er around alone a couple of times, Don. I'd like to stretch my legs awhile." Without waiting for Don's joyous reaction, Ben Mills turned his back and strode, grinning, toward his daughter.

Debbie waved happily to Don. She knew that she was sharing one of his biggest moments.

Don turned the Cub around and taxied to the end of

the runway. Holding the brakes, he ran up the engine, checking its ignition. Then he looked carefully for incoming planes, swung onto the strip and took off.

He made two wide circles at about fifteen hundred feet, executing his turns smoothly. He then established another well-planned approach, touched down easily, and returned to the apron. "How'd I do?" he shouted, leaping to the ground.

"Wonderful!" Debbie cried.

"Very good, Don," her dad said. "Congratulations!"

"Boy! That front seat sure did look empty to ol' Don!"

Debbie's dad laughed. "From now on, you'll be sitting in it!"

Don grabbed Debbie's hands and whirled around with her in a ridiculous dance. "How'd you like that landing—pretty neat, huh?"

"The best!" Debbie happily agreed.

"Wings fit ol' Don just fine!" he chortled.

"Let's celebrate," Debbie said eagerly. "Let's go to Pearson's for a malt!"

"Take our car, Deb," her father said quickly, "so that Don can return theirs—and the malts are on me." He gave Don a dollar from his billfold.

"Thanks, Mr. Mills!"

They took the back booth at Pearson's. Not that it offered more privacy; but it was farthest from the juke box, and so it was possible to talk without shouting. Two other booths were occupied.

Debbie and Don said "Hi," to the others, and Don ordered malts—strawberry for Debbie, vanilla for himself. Then he asked, "How about a movie tonight, Deb?"

"I'd love it, Don!" She paused, then added, "I'll come by for you, and you won't have to ask for your parents' car."

"Your dad allowing you to drive now?"

She nodded.

"It's my place to furnish the car," he said.

"I suppose so—under normal circumstances."

"What do you mean by that, Deb?"

"Well, I was in favor of you selling yours to buy flight instruction. Besides, it isn't fair to take your parents' car when they need it; especially after they bought you one."

"I paid for it myself," he said, "out of the fifteen a week I get for piloting a broom around the *Journal* Building."

"I forgot you worked every morning."

"It's not much of a job," he said deprecatingly. "I could get lots more money at a filling station. I do it mostly to please dad."

Debbie smiled. "If the *Journal* Building were to be mine some day, I wouldn't mind sweeping it."

"You sound like Dad." He laughed.

The malts came. They sipped them, and Debbie told him that her cousin Shayna would arrive tomorrow to spend a week or so. "You remember her—she was here Christmas."

Don grimaced. "I remember."

Both his tone and his facial expression touched a nerve of resentment in Debbie. "Everyone can't be perfect," she said. "Shane *tries* to make people like her."

"It's nothing against you, Deb. But when she comes on with that bragging kick, it's kind of hard to like her."

"You don't understand, Don! You're popular and have lots of friends. Can't you imagine how it would be not to have any at all?"

He shrugged and made no reply. Debbie decided to drop the subject.

A few more of the high school crowd had begun to drift in now. Most of them waved, or called "Hi," leaving Debbie and Don to themselves—but not Kay

Winthrop.

When Kay came in and spotted them, she headed directly for the back booth. She scooted uninvited onto the seat beside Debbie. "This looks like a conspiracy to me!" she said brightly.

"Hello, Kay," Debbie said.

"Have a malt?" Don inquired. Debbie noted that he did not seem unhappy at Kay's intrusion.

Kay giggled, pointing at Debbie's drink, "A pretty pink one? No, thanks. Just a coke, Don."

"We were sort of celebrating," Debbie said, forcing a smile. "Don made his first solo flight today."

"How thrilling!" Kay propped her elbows on the table and, cradling her chin, gazed at Don admiringly. "He can do anything, and is the first all-state halfback Twin Lakes ever had!"

Don smoothed his left eyebrow with the heel of his hand. "Anyone would have looked good behind the kind of blocking the team gave me all season."

"Modest!" Kay purred.

Don smiled at Kay and sipped his malt. It seemed clear to Debbie that he was enjoying Kay's flattery. "The cheer leaders deserve a lot of credit," he said. "They gave the team a lot of spirit." Kay, of course, was a cheer leader.

Kay reached across the table and squeezed his hand. "Thank you, Don. You're sweet to say that." Her inflection made it sound as if he had just proposed to her. Debbie was seething.

Kay picked up her coke and tugged at the soda straw through prettily puckered lips. "My parents are having dinner at your house tonight, Don. They're going to run our vacation films afterwards. Your mother—I'm-crazy-about-her-she's-the-most-considerate-thing—asked that I come, too. Naturally, I told her that I'd love to, if only there would be someone there *my* age."

"I'm sorry, Kay," Don said. "Deb and I planned to go to the movies."

"Oh," Kay said disappointedly. Then she brightened again. "Why don't we all go to your house instead? Three can have more fun than two; and my father is a *scream* feeding the bears in our Yellowstone film!" She turned to Debbie. "How does that sound to you, Debbie? You wouldn't want to be selfish with Don, would you?"

"Yes," Debbie replied coldly.

This was unexpected. For a second or two, Kay was without an answer. Then she laughed. "For a moment I thought you were serious! Hasn't she a wonderful sense of humor, Don?" Kay looked at her watch. "Oh,

I must run!" She slipped from the booth and took Don's hand. "I'll be *so* disappointed if I don't see you tonight—and you too, Debbie. Please take pity on me!"

Debbie and Don were silent for several minutes after Kay had gone. At last Don said tentatively, "She sure makes it hard to refuse her, doesn't she?"

Debbie frowned. "I'd be out of place there, Don, with her parents and all. Also, your mother didn't invite me." She regretted this last sentence almost before it was out, but it was too late to unsay it.

"I know it would be all right if you wanted to come," he said lamely.

Debbie's frown darkened. "All right? I'd be admitted, is that what you mean?"

"Hey, hey, take it easy, Deb! Don't get all shook up over—"

"Who's shook up?" she demanded. "If you want to stay home tonight, it's okay."

"Well, you can see that the whole thing is nobody's fault, actually. Mom expected me to be there, so she asked Kay, figuring it would give me someone to talk to. Mom *is* considerate; that's why I hate to disappoint her."

"Disappoint *whom*?"

"Mom!"

"It's up to you, Don," Debbie said, pushing her malt away.

"No, it's up to you, Deb."

"It's very easy to see what *you* want to do!"

"Now that's not fair, Deb! I'd rather be with you; but a guy owes his mother some consideration."

"Let's call off the movie."

He hesitated, apparently trying to gauge the extent of her resentment. "If we do, will you promise not to be mad?"

Debbie's chin trembled. "Do you expect me to be glad—to send up a flare or something?"

"No, but I expect you to understand, to be a good sport about—"

Debbie's eyes had blurred with tears, and she jumped up, her small fists clenched angrily. "You can just expect something else for a change! Let someone else try a little understanding!" She whirled from the booth and fled. The group around the juke box stared after her.

CHAPTER X

At eleven o'clock the next morning, Debbie heard the distinctive whistling coughs of a Lycoming engine starting outside. She took her purse from the desk and walked out to three-nine-delta. It was time to go to Wichita to meet Shayna.

"Do you want to drive, Deb?" her dad called from the plane.

Debbie nodded, and he slid out to wait for her while she got her pillow from in back and settled into the pilot's seat on the left. Then, with a minimum of swift, sure movements, her hands flicked the knobs and switches that prepare a plane for flight: altimeter set, carburetor heat, mixture, fuel selector, trim—a glance at oil pressure and temperature—and release parking brake. Then she taxied to the runway.

Rolling onto the concrete strip, Debbie pushed the

throttle against the stop, and three-nine-delta leapt forward. Within a few seconds the airspeed indicator swung past fifty, sixty, sixty-five. Debbie deliberately held the plane down, accumulating extra speed—speed that she could convert to altitude at will. Finally she eased the wheel back and allowed the green and white monoplane to seek its element. Her dad turned his face away to hide a pleased smile. "You know, you handle a plane the way a man does, Deb."

Her sober expression did not change. "That's a compliment, Father?"

He opened his mouth to reply, but a glance at her face evidently changed his mind. He watched her from the corner of his eye for a moment. At last he said, "So you and Don had a fight, huh?"

She wound the stabilizer crank a few turns. "Fight?"

He shrugged, then slumped down in the seat to stare out of the window.

Debbie was sorry immediately. He wasn't prying; it was natural for a parent to be concerned. "Yes, Dad, we had a fight. I didn't mean to cut you off like that." She hoped that he would understand. Sympathy was even more useless than regret, and Debbie couldn't bear to be pitied.

He made no reply. Debbie leveled off at three thous-

and and looked sidewise at him. She wouldn't hurt him
for anything. Her dad, too, was covertly looking at
her. She winked solemnly.

He smiled and turned back to the window.

They landed in Wichita twenty minutes later. Then,
after hamburgers and iced tea in the terminal building,
they went outside to meet Central Airline's flight 619
from Oklahoma City and points south.

Shayna emerged from the airliner carrying an over-
night bag and a transistor radio with its volume turned
up to maximum. She was three months younger than
Debbie (her mother was Judith's sister), and was, as
usual, talking to everyone about her. Shayna was much
taller than Debbie, with hazel eyes and light brown
hair (which needed attention). She tugged at the arm
of a dignified lady beside her—obviously a stranger—
and pointed excitedly to Debbie and Debbie's dad.
Then she pushed forward to embrace them.

After the usual, "How are you?" and "How good it
is to see you!" Shayna turned down the volume of her
radio and confided, "It's such a relief to be out of that
plane. Honestly, I don't know what was the matter
with those people!"

Debbie's dad mumbled a sympathetic reply, but it
was lost as Shayna turned up her radio again. He took

her baggage check and went to reclaim her suitcase while Debbie led her cousin to the TriPacer. Returning to Twin Lakes, Debbie's dad sprawled in back while Shayna rode in the co-pilot's seat—clearly impressed that Debbie was in full charge of the plane. Shayna was so impressed, in fact, that she rode most of the forty miles in silence.

But later, helping Debbie to set up the chairs in the hangar for the free movies to be presented that evening, Debbie's cousin returned to normal, and her urge to impress took over. "I hope, Debbie, that the things I brought to wear are appropriate. I simply threw them together; but when one has four closetsful from which to choose, after all—"

"Wish I had that problem." Debbie laughed.

Shayna sighed. "I suppose Mother and Dad would spend a fortune on me if I'd allow it. It's something new every week, and I'll get a new convertible when school starts."

"Golly, you *are* lucky!" Debbie said. "Get a yellow one," she added eagerly; "they're the prettiest!"

Shayna turned down the corners of her mouth. "I told Dad to get me a red one; but it makes no difference really. After all, I mean, when will I ever drive it? Right now I've got five different boys simply *besieging* our house, and all of them have cars!"

Debbie nodded seriously. She knew that Shayna was stretching things. Unless oil had been discovered in the Todds' back yard since Christmas, it was very doubtful that they could afford two cars. Shayna didn't know it, but Debbie had talked to Shayna's mother by long distance phone Christmas eve, and Aunt Helen had said then that it was all they could do to scrape together money enough for Shayna's Christmas visit.

And two years before, Debbie and her dad had stopped to see the Todds when a charter flight took them near the southwest Oklahoma town of Lawton, where Debbie's aunt and uncle lived. Uncle Nat owned a small men's clothing store there. The Todd home had been a very modest place.

Debbie straightened the last row of chairs and looked at her watch. It was two forty-five. She wanted to be around where Don could see her when he came for his lesson at three o'clock. It was only fair to give him a chance, in case he did want to apologize. Besides, a person didn't want to live forever with a sick, empty feeling inside.

"There, the chairs are all fixed," she said to Shayna.. "Shall we get my record player and take it into the office? I have a new Ronnie Beach record."

Shayna made a face. "It's too hot in there. Honestly, how do you exist in this heat without air conditioning?"

"It's nice," Debbie said, "but it's expensive."

"I think I'll have a shower," Shayna said.

"Okay. Or we can go swimming later, if you want to."

"I hate swimming."

"Er—well, we'll find something to do. I'll catch up on my book work while you're in the shower."

Debbie's dad was dozing on the office couch, his feet atop the magazine table. She tiptoed to the desk and eased out the top drawer to get her vanity mirror. She ran a comb through her hair, re-did her pony tail and touched up her lips. Then she checked her watch again. Two fifty-two. He'd be here any minute now.

Her dad stirred. "Is that Don?"

Debbie bent sideways to peer through the window, her pulse quickening. "Yes."

"I'll be in the hangar," her father said. He got up, stretching, and went out.

The outside office door opened, and Don entered. "Hello, Deb." He quickly looked away. "Is—uh—is your dad here?"

"He's in the hangar, Don," she said, her voice carefully controlled.

Don walked across the room, his eyes on the floor, and a sudden panic welled up inside Debbie. *Wasn't he going to talk to her at all?*

But as he reached the door which led into the hangar, he turned. "Deb?"

"Yes?" She knew that she'd answered too anxiously, but she couldn't help it.

"I wish you wouldn't be mad at me." He sounded more defensive than humble.

Debbie turned to the window to stare across the field. "I'm not mad, Don; I'm just hurt."

"You seem pretty mad to me." His voice came from close behind her now.

Debbie watched a grasshopper outside. It made a mighty leap, only to crash against the side of the hangar. "It seemed to me that I suddenly became second choice when your mother arranged an evening with Kay for you." The grasshopper sat quietly in the grass now, contemplating his error.

"You know that you're not second choice, Deb! I felt that I had a duty to Mom, that was all."

The grasshopper tried again. He sailed much higher this time, but struck the wall with a tiny thud, still far below the top. He tumbled ingloriously back to earth, righted himself, hopped away a few feet, then

turned to glare stubbornly at the seemingly insur-
mountable barrier confronting him. Debbie felt a kin-
ship with the little insect, knew how he must feel. She
hoped he made it on his next try. "Yes, Don, you have
many duties to your mother; but I can't believe that
breaking a date with me, in order to be with Kay Winthrop, is one of them."

He was silent for long seconds. At last he said,
"Well, I—at least I'm sorry that your feelings are hurt.
I—well, you know what I mean."

Debbie suddenly realized how terribly difficult it
was for Don to admit that he had been wrong. He
wasn't on his knees, and he wasn't exactly humble; but
a thing offered must be judged according to the circumstances of the offerer. By Carver standards, his was
a most abject apology indeed. Debbie turned and took
his hands. "It's all forgotten, Don." She smiled. "But
please let's not ever go through this again—I've been
miserable!"

"Me, too, Deb," he whispered huskily, pulling her
into his arms.

And for a few seconds Debbie told herself that it
had been worth it. He kissed her then, and she wondered vaguely whether her dizziness came from the
kiss or because he was holding her so tightly. It didn't

matter—nothing did.

A minute later she went to the desk for her handkerchief. "You'd better go, Don. Dad's waiting for you. I'll see you when you land."

"I hate to let you out of my sight that long." He smiled. "But we're only going to Winfield and back." Now that Don had soloed, he had to have a few hours of instruction in cross-country navigation before he could be, as George indelicately put it, "kicked out of the nest." He went out into the hangar, but stopped and stuck his head back inside, "Remember, you promised to be here when I get back!"

"I'll be here," she said. "Shayna came today, you know."

Even this last reminder did not dampen his good humor. He waved cheerily and shut the door. Debbie heard his whistling through the hangar and his happy greeting to her dad. "Hi, Mr. Mills! Sure a beautiful day for flying, isn't it?"

Debbie picked up his tune, humming softly to herself, as she reached for the phone book. She had decided to call as many high school students as she could and personally invite them to the free movies tonight.

After dinner that evening, Debbie's dad dispatched

her to town with the car to pick up some people who lacked transportation but wanted to attend. She made two trips, each time returning five teen-agers to the airport. She knew them all, of course, and was pleased that nearly half of them were girls.

Arriving at the airport with the last carload, Debbie counted seventeen cars parked beside the hangar. If two people came in each, plus the ten she had brought, there might be as many as fifty people there!

It was seven-twenty p.m. and still daylight. All three airplanes and Debbie's glider were neatly lined up on the apron. The visitors milled about them, wiggling tail surfaces, testing seats and peeking into the engine cowls.

George looked strange in a white shirt and tie; sort of professional, Debbie thought, like a doctor or a company president. He circulated among the crowd, answering questions, and reminding everyone that there was plenty of lemonade inside.

Debbie went into the hangar looking for her father. He was adjusting the movie projector. Shayna was sorting film; her transistor radio nearby made talking difficult. "Are you about ready, Dad?"

"Yes. Help George round up everyone."

"I hope we have enough chairs," Debbie said.

"There are quite a few older people out there—Mr. Goodman from the *Journal*, Betty Clarke from the Vogue Shop, and some more."

"That's encouraging," he said.

Debbie turned to go outside and ran into Don. He had brought three boys with him.

"Hi, Deb! Nice crowd. You know these guys, I guess." He gestured to the boys with him.

Debbie did. All were members of the football squad. She welcomed them, then said to Don, "Save me a chair, and one for Shayna, too—Dad's ready to begin."

After everyone was inside, Debbie's father explained that, while the purpose of these sessions was to attempt to interest people in flying, no one was obligated in any way. "Certainly," he concluded, "we don't want this to seem like night school. We hope it is entertaining and fun." The films followed.

Afterwards, Debbie's father spent ten or fifteen minutes answering questions which he illustrated on a portable blackboard. And finally he announced that an attendance record would be kept, and that those present for all four of the weekly movies would be entitled to a free flying lesson.

Everyone was gone before nine-thirty. Don, however, had passed up his ride home (he had come in someone else's car, for the city council met on Tuesday nights, and his father had needed theirs), saying that he had something to tell Debbie. He helped her fold and stack the chairs; then they went into the office while George and Debbie's dad rolled the planes inside. Shayna sensibly remained in the hangar with her radio. Thank heavens for that. Don took Debbie's hand, and they went into the office.

Little thrills ran up her arm from his warm hand, and her heart swelled in anticipation. Now he was really going to say it—tell her right out in words that he loved her!

CHAPTER XI

Debbie switched on the office fan. "It's warm to-night," she said.

"It seemed cool in the hangar, with both ends open."

"We can go outside and sit on the bench," Debbie suggested. It wasn't actually a bench; it was a board supported by a couple of discarded grease pails.

"Okay."

It wasn't much cooler outside, but the silent splendor of the prairie night helped make up for it. "Let's sit in the grass," Don said.

"There are crawly things in the grass," she protested.

"Come on; I won't let anything get you." He sat down, leaning back against the hangar. Debbie slipped down beside him, folding her legs beneath her and resting her head contentedly on his shoulder. He put his arm about her.

"That big star," Don pointed overhead with his free hand, "right up there, is kind of orange."

"That's Arcturus. We're seeing it as it looked thirty-three years ago—that's how long it takes its light to reach us."

"Yeah?" He was silent for a moment. "Then they must be seeing us as we looked thirty-three years ago; and if they are looking at Twin Lakes through a telescope, you and I aren't even here."

"You mean we're not here there," she summed up.

"I do?" His tone was amused.

"Anyway," Debbie said, "Arcturus is a sun. There isn't anyone there with a telescope."

"Maybe it's got some planets circling it, with people with telescopes."

"Um hm," Debbie answered dreamily. She felt his lips brush her forehead. "Your hair smells nice," he said.

She could not resist a secret smile. Maybe a fifteen-cent bar of soap was as good as expensive perfume after all.

"Do you really think there are people out there?" From the sound of his voice, she could tell that he was looking at the stars again.

"Sure."

"You do?"

"Of course. It wouldn't be logical that He'd make billions of suns, yet put an earth with people around only one of them."

"I'd never thought of it that way," Don said. "Maybe, by the time I'm an air force general, I'll go out there and see." He paused. "Er—do you think a guy is crazy to want to do that?"

"No," Debbie said. "The world needs people like that. Otherwise we'd still be living in caves. My dad said that," she added, "when we talked about it once."

He was silent for a time. "I don't know whether the world needs me or not, but I'm going to be somebody, Deb."

Debbie made no reply, waiting for him to continue.

"It's like in football," he went on. "You keep your eyes open, and you learn, and you out-think the opponent, and then you try harder than anyone else, and you win. You win because you deserve to—because you are better than anyone else!" Bless him. He was trying to convince himself as well as her.

"Maybe that sounds snobbish," Don continued, his voice low and urgent, "but that's the most important part! I think it's like my mom has always said: if you expect to be the best, you can't afford to be tolerant of second best. Before anyone else will think of you as *somebody*, you yourself must. And if people call this snobbish—well, it's because they don't understand. It's because they are not striving for high things—because they don't know about the confidence and other things that make a guy hold his head up and be proud inside that he's who he is."

Debbie did not answer at once. At last she said, "I can see what you mean. Also, there's a difference between having confidence in yourself and being snobbish." She recalled that her father had once remarked that he had never known of a truly great person who wasn't humble, but this observation seemed out of place just now, so Debbie didn't repeat it. Instead she asked, "What was it that you were going to tell me, Don?"

"Oh, that. Well, there's going to be another plane out here soon. Dad's leasing a new plane for the *Journal's* use. He says a plane is necessary for an up-to-date newspaper."

Debbie pretended an enthusiasm she did not feel; Don was almost certainly speaking of the plane Mr. Winthrop had purchased. "It sounds wonderful, Don! But why is your father leasing it—why didn't he buy it?"

"It has to do with taxes. Dad says it will cost practically nothing this way, because the yearly lease on it is deductible as business expense."

"Oh," Debbie said, "from whom will he lease it?"

"From Mr. Winthrop," Don said.

"It seems sort of mixed up to me," Debbie said. "How does Mr. Winthrop profit on such a deal?"

"He wants to give Kay some business experience, so he bought the plane in her name. The *Journal* will actually pay Kay for the use of it. It does sound kind of screwy," Don continued, "but, you see, I've been working on Dad to get a plane, and Mom figured out this deal for me because she knew Dad would never buy one, I guess. Mom's my sidekick," he added affectionately. "I think she's the one who sold the Winthrops on the idea."

This last sentence was the one statement that Debbie was willing to accept at face value; of course it had been Mrs. Carver's idea, but there was a great deal more to the whole thing than an innocent business transaction arranged for tax purposes! Of this Debbie was sure. "I've always admired your mother," she said. "I wish I knew her better."

He hesitated for the space of a breath. "Well, why don't you come to dinner at our house some night this week?"

"I'd love to, Don!"

"I'll check with Mom and see which night she and

Dad have free."

"Golly," Debbie said, "I forgot about Shayna. I can't leave—"

"Shayna's invited too, natch."

Debbie's dad stuck his head out of the office window. "I'm buying malts! Any takers out here?"

"Put me in, coach!" Don called.

"Me too!" Debbie added.

They went to Pearson's. There weren't many people in the drugstore at that hour, and the record machine was quiet. Shayna's radio, however, made up for any lack of noise. Debbie's father had a malt with the young people. George drank coffee. They talked of the success of the free movies for a while; then Don asked, "When are you going to try with your glider again, Deb?"

"Maybe day after tomorrow. There's a big low pressure system over lower California on tonight's weather map. If it moves across here, bringing thunderstorm activity, there should be some good thermals ahead of it."

"In that case," Don said, "we'll plan the dinner date for Friday night. That way it'll be a victory celebration in honor of the new women's soaring champion!"

Debbie laughed delightedly, and Shayna leaned

forward eagerly. "Could you take a passenger, Debbie? I mean, your glider has two seats, hasn't it?"

"Golly, Shane, I don't—" She broke off as Tommy Dobbs came up to their booth. "Hi, Tommy."

"This looks like the group with the scoop!" Tommy greeted them airily. "Who's the treasurer for this malt expedition?" Tommy's father was the Ford dealer in Twin Lakes. Tommy was a slender, blond boy; crew-cut, good-natured, and popular at school.

Debbie presented him to her dad and George, then introduced Shayna. "Tommy is our high school tennis champ, Shane."

Shayna said, "Hello," then proceeded to sabotage the "malt expedition" with one of her unthinking attempts at self-eulogy. "You know, our coach at home was *so* disappointed that I stopped playing tennis; but it's such a ridiculous game!"

Tommy looked as if he had been struck in the face. He muttered unintelligibly, declined George's hasty offer of a malt, and left the drugstore. Shayna bent low over her transistor radio, but Debbie could see the desperate regret in the hazel eyes.

"Don," Debbie said quickly, "tell everyone about the plane the *Journal* is going to have." She glanced at Shayna again and felt a surge of sympathy for her.

Shayna meant harm to no one. She was merely trying —however foolishly—to gain friends and respect. Debbie promised herself that *she* would be Shayna's friend.

Don had been telling about the new Cessna, and carefully explaining the tax benefits to the *Journal*. Debbie watched him from the tops of her eyes, her cheeks drawn in with the effort of coaxing the thick malt through a single straw, and decided that maybe Don suspected nothing. He seemed to think that it was a simple business transaction—with no strings attached.

Evidently Debbie's dad did, too. "This sounds like good news to me," he said. "Several businesses in town could profitably use an airplane. Your father is to be congratulated for leading the way, Don."

George frowned at his coffee and said nothing.

Later, preparing for bed, Debbie offered to roll her cousin's hair. Shayna sat at Debbie's dressing table, prattling about the boys who kept her phone busy, as Debbie worked in silence.

If only she could tell Shayna! If only she could say, "Golly, Shane, you don't need to make up all that stuff—people would like you just for yourself if you'd let them!" But Debbie couldn't say it. She put on her pajamas and slipped into bed. " 'Night, Shane."

CHAPTER XII

Debbie was up and dressed shortly after six o'clock Wednesday morning. Her dad was already in the air with a student. He had two farmer-students, who considered the day half gone at that hour. Shayna remained in bed, sleeping soundly.

Debbie went about her normal routine. She went into her father's room, made the bed, shook out the throw-rug and ran the dust mop over the floor. She then went into the kitchen.

On the kitchen table, her dad had left an empty cereal bowl, half a cup of coffee and a note with a twenty-dollar bill attached: DON'T FIX BREAKFAST FOR ME—EXPECT TO BE BUSY THIS MORNING —IF DINNER DATE DON MENTIONED IS AT CARVERS', BETTER TAKE CAR AND GET NEW DRESS—LOVE, FLASH MILLS.

Debbie chuckled, folded the bill and put it into her shoe temporarily. She placed a load of clothes in the washing machine, went in to awaken Shayna, then returned to the kitchen to prepare their breakfasts.

When Shayna appeared, Debbie exclaimed at how pretty she looked. Shayna fluffed the back of her hair self-consciously, then sat at the table in sort of a happy daze. Debbie wondered how long it had been since Shayna had received a compliment.

A little after eight, the two girls walked through the hangar. "Hi, George," Debbie greeted the old mechanic. "Need anything from town?"

"Morning, Miss Debbie, Miss Shayna. Better check the post office box if you all are goin' in. I was late this morning and didn't have time to stop—dad-burned black spot takin' my roses!" When George wasn't at the airport, he could usually be found working on his flower beds at home.

"Golly, I hope you can stop it," Debbie said. "George raises the most beautiful roses in the state of Kansas, Shane," she said to her cousin.

"Put some on your desk," the old man said.

"Thanks, George," Debbie said fondly. "Did you bring this morning's *Journal*?"

"It's in the office; but I didn't see no feature article about the airport in it."

"I forgot to tell you, Mr. Carver is saving it until he sees how well we do with the movies and the fly-in breakfasts."

"Humph!" George snorted. "He's prob'ly savin' it for the wastebasket."

"You wait and see," Debbie said. "I'll bet you he prints it!"

"Maybe so, Miss Debbie—but I got a hunch Clara's goin' to have somethin' to say about it."

"Well, we had a nice crowd last night, whether the paper mentions it or not."

"Sure did," he agreed.

The girls went into the office, and Debbie checked the schedule board while Shayna took an appreciative smell of the flowers George had brought. There were two new names listed as beginning students. Debbie had seen them talking with her father at the end of the class last night. One of them was Betty Clarke of the Vogue Shop.

Debbie left a note for her dad, thanking him and saying that she and Shayna would be back before eleven. Then the two girls went out to the car. It would be nine o'clock by the time they checked the post office, and the stores would be open by then. Shayna had apparently forgotten to bring her radio, for which Debbie was thankful.

As they halted for the traffic light at the city limits, Shayna said, "You know, I thought that boy—what was his name, Tommy?"

"Tommy Dobbs?"

"Yes—the one you introduced me to last night—I thought he was nice, but he didn't seem to like me very well."

"I think he may have misinterpreted what you said about tennis, Shane."

"I don't see why!" Shayna said stubbornly. "He's probably jealous to think that a girl might play as well as he does!"

Debbie groped for some kind of a reply. Then an impatient honk came from behind; the light had turned green. She quickly drove on.

"It doesn't really matter," Shayna went on. "Heaven knows I'm popular enough at home! One male acquaintance more or less won't be noticed." But the note of despair in her voice clearly said that it *did* matter very much.

"Boys are strange creatures sometimes," Debbie said, not knowing what else to say.

They parked in front of the Vogue Shop; but before getting out of the car Debbie saw that the man next to them was preparing to leave. She waited until he'd backed from the curb and driven away; then she quickly moved into the space just vacated. There were almost forty minutes remaining on that meter.

Shayna thought this very amusing. "Really, Debbie,

you're not *that* hard up!"

"I hate parking meters!" Debbie said. "I can't see where you get anything for your money."

They walked the block and a half to the post office. Debbie emptied the box, but did not inspect the mail because Sammie Goodman came in just then to deposit a letter. "Hi, Sammie!"

Sammie joined them and was introduced to Shayna. "I wish I'd come to the airport last night," Sammie said. "Daddy told me about it, and I know I'd have enjoyed it."

"I noticed you weren't there," Debbie said. "Be sure and come next Tuesday."

Sammie sighed. "It makes the second time within a week that Mr. Carver has killed a story of Daddy's —the first one was about you helping those men in that wreck. Daddy was fit to be tied! He says personal prejudice has no place in honest journalism." Sammie glanced over her shoulder at the clerk in the stamp window, who was hanging on her every word. "Let's go outside."

On the sidewalk, Sammie continued, "I don't like to put my nose into other people's personal affairs, Debbie, but we are friends, and there's something else I think you might like to know."

Debbie nodded silently, waiting for Sammie to go on.

"Well, prepare yourself for a shock. Yesterday Mr. Carver told Daddy that Ben Mills' daughter was a fine, intelligent young woman! Can you imagine? I mean, everyone down at the *Journal* knows that the Carvers have been against you and Don going together —at least that's the rumor. And now Daddy says it makes him believe that it's Mrs. Carver who ordered those stories killed!"

Debbie was quiet for a few seconds. "I'm glad to know about it, Sammie," she said. "Thanks for telling me."

"I kind of thought it would be important," Sammie said. "And gee, Debbie, you know the Goodmans are pulling for you!"

"Thanks," Debbie said, smiling. "Like General Custer said, 'I propose to fight it out on this line if it takes all summer.'"

Sammie had no reply for this; she was an "A" student in history.

Returning to the airport an hour later, Debbie's morale had risen slightly. She had found—in the Vogue's bargain rack—the exact dress she wanted. It was a short-sleeved print in brown and yellow, with a full skirt. And by adding four dollars from her own money, she had been able to get a pair of bone shoes that matched the dress perfectly.

Debbie parked beside the hangar and, sharing the grocery sacks and the Vogue packages with Shayna, went through the hangar. George was refueling the Cub on the apron. Her dad was probably in the office.

Leaving Shayna to put away the groceries, Debbie returned to the car for the mail. Sorting through it, she discovered an air mail letter addressed to her. It was from the *Soaring Society of America,* and marked, "Important." She stopped to open it, but her eye was caught by the return address on an envelope sticking out beneath. This one was from the *Aircraft Mechanics' Association* and had George's name on it. Debbie ran across the apron. "George! George! I'll bet this is you-know-what!" She waved the letter excitedly.

"Just a minute." He completed his task while Debbie stood first on one foot, then the other. At last he stepped down and hung up the gasoline hose. "All right; let's see what we've got."

He took the letter and read it slowly, his lips silently forming each word. There was no change in his expression as he finished. He thrust it back at her and turned away without speaking.

". . . Regret that your candidate for 'Flight Operator of the Year' was not chosen. . . ." Debbie read no farther.

George raised the Cub's engine cowl and poked his head inside. "I thought it would be a couple of weeks yet before they picked one."

"Don't you feel badly, George; you did your best!"

He extracted the oil dipstick and squinted at it through his thick glasses. "Don't know why I was so set on it, Miss Debbie. Should have known it was a long chance all the time."

Debbie leaned close to his ear. "We're a long way from beaten!" she whispered.

The old mechanic managed a grin. "You bet, Miss Debbie! Why, we got more ideas than they had at the world's fair!"

"You bet!"

Debbie went into the office with the balance of the mail. Her father was sitting on one edge of the desk, smiling faintly, as Betty Clarke exclaimed rapturously over her first flying lesson.

". . . So easy to guide! I had no idea—" She turned to Debbie. "Can you imagine, Debbie? I had never been in an airplane before in my life! Yet I turned it without a speck of help—didn't I Ben? —and even guided it down almost to the ground!"

Debbie smiled. "In a month or so, you'll think nothing of going to Chicago or Denver for a weekend," she said.

"Imagine!" Miss Clarke held her brand-new pilot's logbook proudly in both hands. "Same time tomorrow, Ben?" she asked in a soft tone Debbie had never heard her use before.

"Yes, same time, Betty."

So! After one lesson it was "Ben" and "Betty!" Debbie waited until Miss Clarke had gone, then said, "You'd better watch her; I think she's got her eyes on you!" She meant it jokingly, but her father did not smile. He put out his hand for the mail and said nothing.

A second later he returned an envelope to her. "Here's one for you, Deb."

"Oh, I forgot!" She tore it open. Then, unfolding the letter, she gasped in amazement. Attached to the letter was a silver pin which featured three soaring gulls encircled within a wreath. She recognized it immediately as the International Silver "C" award for glider pilots. There were only four hundred holders of this coveted badge in the entire United States!

Debbie read the letter without taking a breath. It

explained that a recent flight of hers had been brought to the society's attention by her father. The facts pertaining to this flight had also been verified by the Kansas Highway Patrol. The letter went on to state that, although the Silver "C" had heretofore been awarded for flights of no less than five hours duration, (plus the required distance and altitude gain), evidence in the society's possession indicated that this flight would have unquestionably exceeded this minimum, except for Debbie's unselfish action, prompted by another's critical need.

The letter concluded that the *Soaring Society of America* considered her conduct to be typical of the high standards expected in motorless flight, and that she had reflected honor upon sailplane pilots everywhere.

Debbie sniffled and, lacking words to express herself, mutely handed the letter to her dad.

He read it carefully. Then he took the little silver pin and unfastened the clasp on back. "You'll probably think I'm corny, Deb, but I'd like to pin this on you myself."

She smiled through misty eyes and stood very straight before him. "Who cares if it's corny?"

"Sure makes me proud," he said.

CHAPTER XIII

Shortly after lunch, Debbie was bent over the old roll-top desk posting the ledger. The electric fan swung back and forth, tugging maliciously at the papers she had pinned down with the discarded engine part. Through the office window she could see heat waves wriggling above the concrete runway. Shayna was on the leather couch, toying with her radio, and talking back to an unsuspecting dee-jay.

Earlier, before noon, a factory pilot had delivered Kay's plane. It sat, its aluminum skin chrome-shiny in the sun, at the far edge of the apron. Debbie had not gone near it.

A quick flash of yellow outside the window told Debbie that her father was landing with a student. A few minutes later he came inside, signed the student's logbook and asked Debbie to give the man a receipt.

This man, the operator of an auto supply store downtown, was the third new customer attracted by the free movies of the night before.

After the auto supply man had gone, Debbie's dad studied the schedule board for a minute, then came back to the desk. "Have you been listening to the weather reports, Deb?"

She shook her head. "I haven't had time, Dad."

"There was high cirrus early this morning, and now we have alto-cumulus clouds. A few minutes ago, I noticed that the barometer had dropped sharply. I'd say that weather system you were watching has speeded up quite a bit."

Debbie went to the door and scanned the western sky. She returned thoughtfully. "It'll be here before dark," she said.

"I can cancel Don—he's my only appointment this afternoon—and give you a tow in your glider if you want to take advantage of this condition."

"It's pretty late to start a long flight," she said doubtfully. "However, you just tow me into the air—I'll stay up there until someone has to come after me!"

He chuckled and squeezed her shoulder affectionately. "I believe that!" he said. He went to the door leading into the hangar, then turned back. "We'll transfer the oxygen equipment from three-nine-delta to your glider so you can ride those big thermals all the way to the top. I'm going to tag along in the Cub and keep you in sight."

"Only thing," she said, "if I have any luck at all, you'll run out of gas before I come down."

"I can stop for gas along the way and then catch up again."

"We'll have to go southeast to stay ahead of the storm and to keep off the airways."

"Okay." He came back across the room. "But let me make one thing clear, Deb. Take no chances. Avoid places where turbulence is likely. Another thing: keep your 'chute harness buckled. I've noticed that you've been careless about this lately; but if you ever have to leave your glider in a hurry, you won't have time to stop and dress!"

"Roger. But after scrimping for two years to pay for it, it would be pretty hard to leave it and watch it crash."

"I'm not worried about that," he said. "I can tell you, it's not hard to use your rag-bag when it's the only way out—too bad they don't have something like it for cars."

"I'd better call Don," she said. "He—" She stopped

and bent forward to look through the window as a car drove up outside. "Well, there he is now!"

"He's early. It's only one-twenty."

Debbie went to the door to greet Don, but he was not on his way in. He was walking across the apron toward Kay's plane—and Kay was tripping along beside him. The Winthrop Thunderbird was parked behind the Carver sedan.

Debbie's first impulse was to turn back inside and slam the door; but she thought better of it. She summoned the sweetest smile at her command and started across the concrete apron to join them.

They had not seen her, and Debbie almost caught up to them when she heard Don say, "It's beautiful, Kay! A beautiful thing! Some day I'm going to have one like it."

"Would this one do?" Kay asked quickly.

"Huh?"

"It comes complete with co-pilot," Kay said coyly.

Debbie forced herself to remain quiet, waiting for Don's reply. He merely smoothed his eyebrow nervously with the heel of his hand.

Then Kay saw Debbie. "Hi, Debbie." If Kay had a guilty conscience, it did not show.

"Hello," Debbie replied coldly.

"Hi, Deb!" Don said apprehensively.

"Hello, Don. I hope you'll forgive me; I couldn't resist eavesdropping on such a tempting offer!"

Kay laughed. "Doesn't her sense of humor simply *kill* you, Donny?"

Evidently it didn't; Don wasn't laughing. "I—uh—we came out to see the *Journal's* new plane, Deb," he said, obviously wishing he were somewhere else.

Debbie smiled faintly and made no answer.

"It's nice, don't you think?" he asked tentatively.

"Very nice," Debbie agreed with elaborate politeness.

"I was hoping your dad would check me out in it. I'm supposed to fly it for the paper, you know."

"I know," Debbie said gravely. "Now will you excuse me? My father is waiting." She walked back to the office with as much dignity as her impatient legs would allow.

Shayna was waiting in the office doorway. "Could I go with you, Debbie?" she asked urgently.

"Shane, I must save every ounce that I can. Besides, it may be a long and tiring flight. If Dad and I aren't back before dark, George will stay here with you."

"Well, I hoped that maybe—I mean, I just know that you're going to make a record—George says you're the best there is—and if I could only be with you, I—" Shayna lowered her gaze self-consciously. "To tell the truth, Debbie, I'm not quite as popular at home as I've been pretending. Somehow I don't seem to click with—well, what I'm trying to say is, if I could only sort of help do something worth-while, then maybe—" She looked up imploringly. "You *do* understand, don't you?"

Debbie's heart went out to her. Shayna's weight could mean the difference between success and failure; but Debbie could not look at the lonely, wounded girl and refuse. "Okay, Shane, if you'll promise to stick it out, no matter what. I can't land if you get airsick or anything."

"I won't be any trouble, honest! I'll *help*."

Debbie smiled and squeezed her cousin's hand. "Well, friends should stick together," she said. "Go change to your pedalpushers, and bring a sweater."

"Oh, gee, Debbie! You're super!" Shayna hugged her excitedly, then dashed from the office. Debbie followed, to change her own clothes.

When the girls appeared on the flight line a few minutes later, the sailplane had been moved outside. Debbie's dad and George were securing the oxygen tank behind the front seat. Don was standing beside the glider, absently stroking the wing's smooth leading edge. Kay's Thunderbird was gone.

Debbie's dad was shocked to learn that Shayna intended to go along. "I don't think Shayna would mind waiting until another time, Deb; and the extra weight greatly increases the odds against you."

"Odds, Father?" Debbie replied with a straight face. "Haven't you ever heard of the Battle of Midway?"

"Guess that'll hush you, Ben," George said.

"You count to something if you have to use this, don't you?" Shayna asked nervously.

"Forget about countin', Miss Shayna," George said. "Just say the Lord's Prayer. When you get to 'hallowed be Thy name,' pull that ring there."

"George," Debbie scolded, "you shouldn't joke about the Lord's Prayer!"

"Who's jokin' Miss Debbie?"

"We forgot the thermos," Debbie said, checking the front cockpit.

"I'll go get it!" Shayna said, and ran for the apartment, the heavy 'chute bumping against her legs.

"I'll get the Cub," Debbie's dad said, "if Don will help push the glider out to the strip."

"Sure, Mr. Mills!"

A couple of minutes later, Shayna arrived with the thermos, and the girls got into the sailplane. Don bent forward eagerly to help Debbie fasten her seat belt and shoulder harness. George performed a similar rite for Shayna.

Don pecked Debbie lightly on the forehead. "Good luck, Deb," he whispered.

"Thanks, Don." Then she smiled. "I'll be back in time for our dinner date tomorrow night—that is, if you haven't traded me for an airplane in the meantime."

The blue eyes clouded for an instant; then he straightened up and matched her smile. "I'm waiting for a better offer," he said.

Debbie stuck out her tongue at him, then turned to explain the oxygen mask to her cousin.

Then, as her father hooked onto the towline downfield, she closed the canopy and wiggled her fingers in farewell.

A few seconds later, the sleek silver craft had come alive, and they were twenty feet above the runway, with the soft hiss of air squeezing through the side vent bringing relief from the sweltering heat. Once again Debbie's heart seemed to gain buoyancy with her wings, and earth-troubles—things which did not belong in the sky—fell away below.

At three thousand feet, Debbie increased back pressure on the control stick to draw the towline taut. She tripped the tow release and banked steeply away to the right. The usual "bang," not unlike a rifle shot, came a split-second after the line was dropped—but this time it was immediately followed by a strange popping sound. Debbie had no idea what it could be, though she knew that it wasn't normal. She lowered the nose and leveled the wings, then looked back at Shayna.

Shayna was staring at the left wing, her hazel eyes round with apprehension. She pointed wordlessly, and Debbie twisted in her seat to follow her cousin's finger.

There was a great dent in the aluminum leading edge of the wing, and a narrow strip of fabric had peeled back from it to whip in the wind! A varnished wing rib showed nakedly from beneath the rent skin! Debbie knew immediately what had happened. The heavy metal eyelet at the end of the towline had somehow been given a dangerous flick at the instant of release and had struck the wing!

Now don't get excited, Debbie! she admonished herself. *Think*—don't panic! She forced herself to study the damage calmly, realizing that the gravest emergency had passed; if the wing had been damaged sufficiently to cause it to go completely, it would have ripped away by now. Debbie was familiar with every piece inside the wing, because she had watched impatiently throughout the winter and spring as George assembled it in the back of the hangar. And it was evident now that there was no internal structural damage—the wing was as strong as ever. The slit in the fabric, plus the dented front edge, would subtract from the glider's performance; however, there seemed to be no real danger.

The question now was, should she continue, or should she land and try again after repairs had been done? Trouble was, the perfect soaring conditions existing today might not be repeated again this year, at least not before school started. If she hoped to be considered for the U.S. Soaring Team, she must prove herself now, or perhaps never.

Then suddenly her mind was made up for her. She had stumbled into an extra-strong thermal that soon had her variometer registering nineteen hundred feet per-minute ascent. It was the kind of updraft that no glider pilot could resist if he had as much as a discarded billboard to ride. Debbie turned back to Shayna. "That's nothing serious, Shane! Everything is okay!"

Shayna glanced doubtfully at the left wing, then nodded weakly.

Debbie turned forward, then smiled to herself as she noted that her left hand gripped the canopy release. She had not been aware of it. Subconsciously, in a crisis, she had been prepared to bail out. Her dad was right: if necessary, the rag-bag was not hard to use!

At nine thousand feet, the thermal cooled and lost much of its life. Clouds were forming, and the outside air temperature was fifty-six degrees. It was not unpleasantly cool, however, for the sun was high and made a veritable greenhouse of the Plexiglas-canopied cockpit. Debbie banked onto a southerly heading, searching for her father.

She located him a couple of thousand feet below and a mile to the east. She exchanged wing waggles with him, then edged eastward toward one of the flock of cloud sheep crowding the sky ahead.

As the girls swung beneath the cloud, the variometer began racing up the scale: Eight hundred, fourteen hundred; at last indicating twenty-two hundred feet per-minute ascent! Within seconds they were swallowed by the cool, gray dampness of the cloud, and for a minute or two, Debbie flew on instruments alone: turn-needle, one width, ball-bank indicator, centered; air speed, sixty miles per hour and steady. Then they burst into blinding sunlight above, flung from the upward-building cloud as a stone is hurled from a slingshot. Water droplets whipped from the trailing edges of the wings and blurred forward vision through the canopy. The altimeter had swung past fourteen thousand feet. Debbie put on her oxygen mask and motioned for Shayna to do the same. The torn left wing looked just as it had a few minutes before; Debbie decided to stop worrying about it.

CHAPTER XIV

A minute or so past three p.m., Debbie and Shayna passed high above the Arkansas City Airport. According to the air chart, this field was almost bisected by the Kansas-Oklahoma State Line. The girls were at seventeen thousand feet now, and had worn their oxygen masks since riding that first infant thunderhead to fourteen thousand. From this height, the airport below was hard to find. Even Arkansas City itself, a medium-sized town a mile or so to the north, was ridiculously tiny.

Debbie's dad, mindful of his rule not to go above twelve thousand without oxygen, had remained below. Debbie saw him balance the Cub on a wing tip and fall away toward the distant earth. He was undoubtedly taking advantage of the chance to refuel, with an airport so handy.

The line of thunderstorms was well developed behind them, and was growing rapidly around the western and southern horizon. It was foolish to play with these awesome giants once they had matured, so she swung eastward a few more degrees and edged away from the crowding storm cells. The Arkansas River, inching below the left wing and uncoiling toward Tulsa, made navigation easy.

At four o'clock, Tulsa was visible twenty miles or so to the east. Debbie's dad had caught up with the glider again, and they flew side by side at nine thousand feet. They were approximately one hundred and twenty miles from Twin Lakes, which meant that eighty-one miles remained to equal the present record. The current Women's Distance Record of two hundred and one miles had stood since 1952, which was evidence enough that only an unusual combination of skill and good fortune should better it.

The girls had taken off their oxygen masks, so Debbie passed the thermos to Shayna. "Will you pour me a sip in the lid, Shane?"

Her cousin nodded. "Where are we—what is that over there?" She pointed to Tulsa.

Debbie told her, and answered other questions about altitude and speed. "Are you getting tired?"

Shayna shook her head. "It's too beautiful. I got a little cold, though, when we were higher." She handed Debbie a cupful of iced tea.

Debbie emptied and returned it. "We've done well so far; but keep your fingers crossed for a couple more hours."

"It seems so easy and effortless," Shayna said. "I can't see what would keep us from going a thousand miles!"

"No danger of that!" Debbie laughed. "When that storm front covers the sun, we'll be out of business!"

"Is it as close as it looks?"

"It's close enough," Debbie said. And as if to punctuate her words, the glider's wings rocked sharply as they passed through an area of turbulence. Debbie swung the nose another degree or two eastward.

Funny thing about the wind noise, she thought. It sometimes seemed to repeat a phrase over and over, similar to the clicking rhythm of train wheels. Now Debbie was almost certain that she could detect music in it—a melody. Then, suddenly, the truth dawned, and she whirled in her seat to discover the inevitable: Shayna had slipped her transistor radio aboard!

For a second Debbie was angry. Didn't Shayna realize that every ounce was a liability? No, of course she didn't. Debbie sighed resignedly. There was no point in scolding Shayna; the damage was done.

Besides, greater problems needed attention. Thunderheads were forming to the east, and except for the narrow hall of clear sky ahead, they were completely encircled by the storm.

An hour later, they were coasting at twelve thousand feet. Debbie turned her head about slowly, enchanted by the immense storm clouds. A tiny tremor ran down her spine. She felt as if she were an ant in a cathedral. The awesome thunderheads surrounding them were vaulted corridors of incredible magnificence. Treading these footless halls, a mere human could only become overwhelmed with a sense of insignificance.

It was after five o'clock, and during the past hour Debbie had been busy. A great chunk of the nine thousand feet so confidently possessed just sixty minutes before had been drained away when the glider had been caught in a cold mass of air spilling down the sides of the encroaching storm.

Fortunately, Debbie had located another thermal before being forced to land, and once again she was, as George would say, "fat with altitude." Nevertheless, she had made but twenty miles headway during

the past hour. They were still sixty-one miles short of
the two-hundred-and-one-mile record—and the lifting
air was becoming harder to find.

At intervals, the lowering sun split the tremendous
cloud walls and sent dazzling shafts of light across
the changing frescoes of mist; their rainbow colors,
slanting between the thousand foot walls, heightened
the illusion that they shone through great stained-glass
windows. But the path of clear air was narrowing. It
had long since roofed over solidly above. Several
hundred feet off the glider's right wing, Debbie's dad
kept pace.

Thirty minutes later, Debbie was desperate. She
had steadily lost altitude until now the altimeter had
but a mere eight hundred feet to report. They were
over farmland, a few miles east and north of Holden-
ville, Oklahoma, according to the chart. They were
also short of a record by approximately thirty-five
miles.

Then, at the point of conceding defeat and choosing
a landing spot, Debbie found a flicker of hope in the
distance—a prairie hawk, circling in search of a meal.
But even as she banked toward him, she knew that
she could never reach his thermal before running out
of altitude—unless—she turned excitedly to Shayna.

"Can you unbuckle the oxygen tank, Shane? Hurry!"

Shayna bent forward to tear at the straps holding the heavy cylinder behind Debbie's seat. "I can get it, Debbie!"

"Throw it out, quick!"

Debbie opened the canopy while her cousin tugged the unwieldly steel drum to the cockpit's edge and allowed it to tumble overboard. "Anything else that's loose!" Debbie cried over her shoulder. "We only need a few more miles, Shane!" Debbie sent the thermos into the slipstream next, then her old brown-and-white loafers—even the air charts!

Relieved of many pounds, the sailplane held a new buoyancy that Debbie could feel in the controls. Now they might make it to the updraft before their last eight hundred feet of altitude was gone.

It was close. It was very close. They picked up the ascending column of air over a little patch of scrub-oak less than a hundred and fifty feet above the ground. It was a good thermal, though probably the last they would find. At four thousand feet, just below cloud base, it died. The sun was gone. Soon the storm would take the land.

Twenty minutes later, Debbie rocked her wings at her dad and turned into a downwind pattern for a landing. She had chosen a large pasture near a farm-house. A few drops of rain were spreading in wind-blown patterns on the canopy. She did not know whether or not they had established a new record. The charts were gone. They could be a mile or two short, or a mile or two over.

They touched down in the short-cropped grass, braking to a stop as a man and woman hurried from the nearby farmhouse. Debbie's dad circled once, then followed the glider down. Debbie had chosen this field with the Cub's landing requirements in mind. Her father climbed from the Cub to join her and Shayna as the farmer and his wife arrived. The farm couple were middle-aged, plainly but neatly dressed, and with pleasant faces.

"My land, Curtis," the farmer's wife whispered loudly, "two of them are girls!"

Debbie's dad stepped forward, smiling, and offered his hand to the farmer. He introduced himself, his daughter and niece, then explained what they were doing there.

"If we can be of any help, just say so, Mr. Mills!" Curtis offered.

"Thanks," Debbie's dad replied. "A storm is about to break, so the girls and I had better tie down our aircraft." He trotted to the Cub and brought out the rope and stakes.

"Curtis, you give them a hand there," the farmer's wife said. "And you folks come inside as soon as you get finished. She turned to leave. "I've got biscuits in the oven."

"We can stay in our planes, ma'am," Debbie's father said. "We don't want to cause you any trouble."

"Nonsense! I won't hear of such a thing! You and the girls come in—it's 'most suppertime!" She peered closely at the sailplane, then turned to Debbie, "This one hasn't got any propeller—is it a jet?"

"No, ma'am. It's only a glider."

"My land!" She hurried away toward the house. "The young'uns sure skit around these days!"

After the planes were secured, Debbie got air charts from the Cub; and following a slight delay due to a rocky patch of ground, over which the two men were forced to transport the shoeless girls piggyback, they made it to the house ahead of the storm.

Debbie was anxious to establish their exact location —any place on earth was fine, if it were more than two hundred and one miles from Twin Lakes—but courtesy dictated that she and Shayna offer to help with the supper. The storm left them no choice but to stay and

eat. Besides, the aroma of smoked ham and hot biscuits was a pretty strong argument in itself.

The farmer's wife (who insisted that everyone call
her "Effie") assigned the gravy to Debbie; Shayna
was put to chopping lettuce for a salad; and Effie
filled another pan with biscuit dough and sliced off
more ham.

Debbie's dad came in and spread the chart on the
kitchen floor. Curtis stood behind, watching curiously,
as Debbie's father carefully measured their distance
from Twin Lakes. He went through the ritual twice
before getting up to announce: "One hundred and
ninety-seven and a half miles, Deb."

She was transfixed with disappointment. "I—are you
sure?" she wailed.

"Afraid so. You'll have to be satisfied with just *one*
record this time."

It required several seconds for this to register.
"What do you mean?" she asked carefully.

Her father was finding it difficult to keep a straight
face. "The record for a flight *with passenger* was, until
a few minutes ago, one hundred and seventy and a
third miles!"

There was a moment of open-mouthed silence; then
Debbie's dad was smothered by a pair of laughing,

squealing, deliriously happy girls.

"Hear that, Curtis?" Effie beamed. "The girls made a record!"

Curtis sniffed the unattended gravy. "Make mighty fine gravy, too," he said.

"Just think," his wife said, "a record—right out there in our pasture!"

"Beats all," Curtis agreed. "Supper about ready?"

"Yes." Effie sighed. "Sit down. Mr. Mills, you sit here. Debbie, I'll bowl the gravy. You sit over there; Shayna, you at the end—my land! Listen to that rain come down!"

"Something else you'll be interested to know," Debbie's father said as the girls subsided into their designated places. "Your record is official."

"But how—" Debbie was speechless for the second time with half a minute.

"George knew where to borrow a barograph in Wichita." Her dad grinned. "I picked it up when I went after the films. It's bolted behind the back seat right now!"

"We'll be famous!" Shayna cried, as Debbie bit back happy tears.

So, despite Effie's marvelous buttermilk biscuits, the succulent smoked ham and candied yams, Debbie and

Shayna had little appetite remaining. They talked excitedly of their flight while the others ate.

"Do you think I helped?" Shayna asked.

"Golly, yes!"

Shayna was quiet for a few seconds. "I'll miss my radio," she said softly.

"Shane! You *didn't*!"

"You said every ounce counted. I had to do what I could to help."

CHAPTER XV

At fifteen minutes before seven the following evening, Debbie and Shayna turned into the long curving driveway that led to the Carver house. Debbie inhaled deeply. Sprinklers were making wide sweeps on the lawn, and the air was sweet with the smell of wet freshly cut grass. It was a good smell, so different from the gasoline, airplane dope and sun-baked concrete of the airport.

Don was waiting to greet them. Debbie's heart swelled in pride. How lucky could a girl get? He had on a white dinner coat which contrasted with his tan; framed between the tall columns supporting the upper balcony of his home, he seemed remote—a world away from a girl reared in an airport.

He came down to meet them, opened the car door and took Debbie's hand. "It takes a secret password to get in here tonight, lady!" He grinned.

Debbie pretended to think. "Is it top secret, or just an everyday secret?"

"I'll tell you. The word is 'gorgeous.' But you're not supposed to say it."

"I'm not?" There was a big pink balloon inside her chest where her heart should have been.

Don shook his head. "Nope. You *look* it." His grin spread, and he added, "Pass, Gorgeous."

Debbie laughed, but her eyes stung, goose that she was. Maybe it wasn't so far from the airport to the Carver home, after all.

Shayna came around the front of the car and joined them. "I hope you have an easier password for me, Don."

"Same one!" he said airily, taking each of their arms. "You're both gorgeous."

Shayna giggled and looked up at him gratefully.

They went up the steps and crossed the veranda. "I wanted to cook hamburgers on the patio, but Mom overruled me," Don said.

"You said it was to be informal, so Shane and I dressed accordingly."

"You both look swell."

They entered the tall doorway. Then, a dozen steps

down the hall, Don steered the girls into a high-ceil-inged sitting room. Mrs. Carver was arranging a vase of roses on a marble-topped coffee table. Mr. Carver, who had been frowning at the evening paper, arose and came forward to greet Debbie with unusual warmth.

Don's mother turned, smiling. "Welcome, Deb-orah! And this is Shayna, isn't it?" She hurried across the thick green carpet to take their hands. "We are happy to have you, my dears!"

"It was nice of you to ask us," Debbie said.

"Please sit down. Dinner will be served at seven."

"Thank you." Debbie sat upon a fragile-appearing Early American settee. Shayna eased down nervously beside her.

Don picked up a wing-chair of similar design and moved it close to Debbie. "These things are prettier than the bench at the airport, but not much softer!"

"They're beautiful," Debbie said. "And priceless, too."

Mrs. Carver raised an eyebrow. "Why, Deborah, do you possess a knowledge of antique furniture?"

"If they were in a store, I wouldn't know the dif-ference, Mrs. Carver; but here I do."

"I don't quite follow you, my dear."

Debbie smiled. "I know that you would not have

them unless they were genuine."

Mrs. Carver was pleased in spite of herself. "That is very generous of you, Deborah." She raised her chin a trifle. "I suppose I do have something of a reputation."

"The carpet is lovely, too," Shayna ventured.

Mr. Carver took a chair beside his wife. Debbie had not seen him since the previous Thursday, when she had gone to the *Journal* Building to place the ad. His attitude toward her did seem much friendlier. "I think congratulations are in order, Debbie, for your record flight!"

"Thank you, Mr. Carver. Shane is due much of the credit. It was she who jettisoned the heavy equipment so we could squeeze out those last few miles."

"We even threw our shoes overboard!" Shayna put in.

"How dramatic!" Don's mother said. "Tell me, Deborah, is there a practical reward—I mean, of course, a prize of some sort?"

"Not directly, Mrs. Carver. My reasons for the attempt were to gain certain objectives, however."

"Can you tell us about them?"

Debbie smiled again. "I hope to be considered for a place on the United States Soaring Team which will go to Europe next spring." She hesitated. Did she dare? "The other reason was that the city council requires newsworthy and increased activity at the airport as a condition for renewing Father's lease."

Don's mother continued to smile as though this had absolutely nothing to do with her. She made no reply.

In the brief silence that followed, Don leaned forward to inspect the small silver pin Debbie wore. "I haven't seen that before, Deb. Is it something special?"

"I haven't had time to tell you about it; it came yesterday morning." She went on to explain her Silver "C" in a couple of modest sentences.

"Big deal!" he said admiringly. "Guess ol' Don's going to have to fly high to keep up with you!"

Debbie laughed. "Right now, I'll accept all the praise you'll offer; because you'll be flying jet fighters in a year or so, and then my sailplane will seem like a toy to you!"

"I won't be driving jets that soon," Don said, sobering. "The Air Academy, believe it or not, doesn't have a single airplane!"

"It doesn't?"

Don shook his head. "It's just like college, except it's got drill sergeants in place of house-mothers—five years of college squeezed into four. The guys who survive it are then taken to the airfield and shown a strange object. 'That thing there,' they are told, 'is an airplane. This is the front, and this the back. Now we'll get down to the business you came for in the first place!' "

Shayna laughed, and Debbie said, "Think of the advantage you'll have. You already know which is the front and which the back."

"I probably won't—not by the time I stagger out of the academy, stuffed with formulas and history."

Don's mother was not amused. "Really, Donald, the academy is not to be so disparaged! Colonel Scott explained to you that its objectives are education and leadership; that it seeks to produce superior officers and gentlemen rather than mere fliers!"

"I was only kidding, Mom." Don turned to his father, "Have you talked to Senator Sheppard lately, Dad, about my appointment to the academy?"

"Saw Andy in Wichita last week, Son. He assured me that it is all settled. You know, the Falcons have a great football team, too."

"I know. But it seems to me that if they've got time to play football, they've got time to fly a little."

"There's no reason to belabor that point, Son. Your mother and I consented to your flying lessons here.

While you are in Colorado Springs, you can fly in your off-hours until after graduation."

"I don't see how," Don said.

"Surely, Donald," his mother said quietly, "you are aware that your father and I arranged for this spanking-new plane solely for your benefit." She reached for his hand and pressed it affectionately.

Don smiled uncertainly—almost guiltily, Debbie thought. "Gosh, I thought it was just for the paper's use. I don't know what to say!"

"Don't know what to say" indeed! Debbie thought grimly. She looked at Don's father, but Mr. Carver quickly turned his head. Nor would Don look at her. Well, his parents had certainly foreseen, and very carefully planned—*plotted* was a better word—every detail of Don's future! There was clearly no provision in that future for one Debbie Mills—nor was there any longer a particle of doubt concerning the reason for Kay Winthrop's ownership of the Cessna.

CHAPTER XVI

Entering the dining room, Debbie savored the fragrance of a great bowl of yellow roses which dominated the long table. The room had a quiet, formal feeling; it was the kind of room in which one hesitated to speak loudly. It was large, brown-carpeted, with tall curtains of gold brocade. In the center, the pointed flame-tips of a dozen candles in ornate silver candelabras made a soft light about the table, leaving the rest of the room in twilight.

Mr. Carver seated his wife at one end of the table, himself at the other. Don held high-backed chairs for Debbie and Shayna in turn, then went around to sit across from the girls. He craned his neck to look around the roses at Debbie. "I'm either going to have to get you a dictionary to sit on or move these flowers," he said, grinning.

She smiled at him and turned to his mother. "Mrs. Carver, I have been trying to find words to tell you how much I like your dress."

Don's mother glanced down at the pale-blue net gown that she wore. "Thank you, Deborah. I found it in New York last summer." As an afterthought she added, "Your frock, and Shayna's, too, have aroused my admiration."

Debbie said, "Thank you," and paused apprehensively as her cousin acknowledged the compliment. Only yesterday, Shayna's need to impress could not have passed up such an opportunity, but she merely smiled and moved her lips in a mute "thanks."

Don's father swept the fold from his napkin in a single motion, then attacked his salad. "Speaking of colleges," he said, "what are your plans after high school, Deborah?"

"I hope to go to the University of Kansas, Mr. Carver."

"Now there's a young woman with judgment!" he announced. "That was my school! What will you major in?"

"Meteorology; I've always been interested in weather."

"That seems a rather unusual career for a woman,

Deborah," Mrs. Carver said.

"The career I hope for, Mrs. Carver, is that of homemaker." Debbie smiled at Don and went on, "But to me, weather is fascinating, and I would like to do research in that field—though I would never allow it to interfere with my home and family."

"I thought that we'd pretty well have weather under control with the weather-satellite program," Don's father said.

"The satellites will help," Debbie replied, "especially in long range forecasting; but they won't solve everything. Do you realize, Mr. Carver, that we don't know why tornados form, or even how a raindrop is made?"

"I should think it was all a matter of simple physics."

"But it isn't! Things happen in the upper air that seem impossible! Clouds, for example, made of supercooled water, that are far below freezing temperature, yet don't turn to ice!"

"That *is* interesting," Mr. Carver said. "I thought that water always froze at thirty-two degrees or below."

Debbie shook her head. "Something else is needed. Whatever it is, it is almost always present on earth, but it is often lacking in the sky. My father has flown through such clouds, at altitudes where the temperature was more than thirty degrees below freezing, yet the moisture in the clouds remained in water form! I hope to find some in my sailplane, so that I can study them without a propeller to churn them up."

Mr. Carver pushed his salad away. "It seems to me, Debbie, that you have a pretty good start in this field."

"Golly, Mr. Carver, I don't know very much about it. I only meant that I was interested!" Debbie wanted to bite her tongue for the "golly," but it was too late. She took her salad fork and cut a wedge from the mayonnaise-spread pear half. The salad also had chopped nuts and cherries sprinkled on it.

"I should think the life of a lady forecaster would be quite interesting," Mrs. Carver said.

Debbie continued with her salad and did not reply. She was certain that Mrs. Carver well knew the difference between a forecaster and a research scientist. But realizing that it would be rude not to make some kind of reply, Debbie managed a smile for Don's mother. Then she turned to her cousin. "I've never heard you say, Shane, whether or not you planned a career."

"I'd like to study music," Shayna said, "although

I doubt if I have much talent for it," she added with a laugh.

"Donald, dear, you are not eating your salad," his mother said.

"It's got mayonnaise on it, Mom." Don's tone was one of explanation, not censure. But his mother beckoned to the servant.

"He can leave it, Clara," Mr. Carver said as Robert came forward. "There are plenty of other things."

"Olga knows perfectly well that Donald detests mayonnaise, Milton! Robert, please bring Donald another salad."

"Yes, Mrs. Carver." Robert took the offending dish and went out.

Don's mother turned to her guests and said, "Olga is a dear, really, though she is quite strong-willed at times." Mrs. Carver smiled to show that she was not truly angry with her cook.

Robert returned a minute later with Don's "salad." It was now minus even the lettuce, chopped nuts, and cherries. It consisted of a lonesome half-pear on a dish by itself. Debbie had to bite her lip to keep from smiling. Olga had had the final word.

Mrs. Carver frowned, although she said nothing. Don, however, to his everlasting credit in Debbie's

eyes, chuckled to himself as he ate the bit of fruit.
A boy who could laugh at a joke on himself deserved
to be forgiven a few other things, Debbie decided.

A minute later, Robert served the roast beef and, as
vegetables and sauce followed, Mr. Carver mentioned
Debbie's record flight again. He listened with interest
while Dbbie briefly told about it. His questions indicated that he had read the account that Mr. Goodman
was preparing of the flight.

Over dessert—a green jello dish, with cream and
fruit whipped in—Don said, "I still haven't had that
ride in your glider that you promised, Deb. I'll bet
I could fly it if I had the chance!"

"Of course you could, Don. The only thing, landing approaches will fool you at first, because a glider
has so much more buoyancy than an airplane."

"Yeah," Don laughed, "George says that you have
to practically get out and stomp 'em down!"

Debbie laughed too. "That sounds like George!"

"Why don't you check me out in it tomorrow?"

"Not tomorrow, Don. According to father's schedule
board, you're listed for a three-hour cross-country
solo."

"*No kidding?*" Boy! I finally get turned loose on
my own!"

"Does this mean, Deborah," Mrs. Carver asked carefully, "that Mr. Mills intends to send Donald hundreds of miles alone?"

"Yes, Mrs. Carver; but my father is very conservative in these matters, and if Don weren't thoroughly capable, Father would not assign him a task greater than that required of the average student."

Mrs. Carver seemed to waver between pride and apprehension. "Ah—then, normally, these flights are of less duration?"

Debbie nodded. "Usually two hours or less, Mrs. Carver."

Don's father bent forward. "I take it, Debbie, that this implies that Don is decidedly above average?"

Debbie smiled. "You'd better ask my father about that, Mr. Carver—I'm prejudiced."

"I am, too," Don's father admitted, chuckling.

"Donald does all things well," his mother said, her handsome chin high once again. "Since his childhood, his father and I have constantly striven to imbue him with the principles of excellence—nor have I the slightest doubt that he will be among the top young men of his class at the academy!"

Don, obviously uncomfortable, attempted to pass it off lightly. "This sounds like a meeting of the Don

Carver Fan Club! Now, I've got some autographed pictures I can hand out—there'll be a twenty-five-cent handling charge, of course!"

Debbie pretended to consider. "I'll have to let you know," she teased with a straight face. "After all, I can buy a malt for that!"

"Well, I suppose I could throw in a malt."

"In that case," Shayna joined in, "I'll take one."

Don shook his head sadly. "Some fan club," he moaned.

Mrs. Carver finally smiled uncertainly; it had taken her a second or two to realize that the young people were joking.

Robert refilled the iced tea glasses while they waited for Shayna to finish her dessert. Don took a last gulp and addressed his father. "Noticed Debbie's record wasn't mentioned in tonight's paper, Dad. Saving it for Sunday?"

As Don spoke, Debbie had turned to his mother to offer a compliment on the dinner, thus Debbie saw the quick warning Mrs. Carver's eyes flicked at her husband. Don's mother lowered her gaze almost immediately, aware that Debbie was looking at her. But in that brief instant, Debbie had seen enough to know that the printing of the story of the record flight had already been argued, or at least discussed, by Don's parents. Debbie had not seen an evening paper; there was no delivery to the airport.

"Well, Son, it—ah—was tentatively set for tomorrow morning's edition," Mr. Carver said.

"It's a good thing I wasn't the boss down there last week," Don said indignantly. "Somebody'd be looking for a job! The *Wichita Sun* had all about Deb helping those guys in that wreck, but there was never a line about it in the *Journal*!"

"Yes, Son," Mr. Carver said, glancing at his wife, "I think that was a mistake."

"I'll say!" Don hesitated, then amended, "But on the whole, I'm pretty proud of the *Journal*."

"I'm glad to hear that," his father replied, and got to his feet. "Shall we go into the den?"

Don held his mother's chair as she arose, and his father made a gesture of aiding Debbie and Shayna. The girls declined after-dinner coffee, as did Don. "Just a demitasse for Mrs. Carver and me, Robert," Mr. Carver said. "We'll be in the den."

"Yes, sir."

The den obviously belonged to the men of the house. It was a big, comfortable room with a cork floor and slip-covered maple furniture. Flying and sports maga-

zines were scattered on the coffee table, and several
model airplanes, evidently Don's creations of a few
years past, shared the mantel with a pair of souvenir
footballs and a small gold trophy.

Debbie went to the mantel and inspected the models.
She did not touch them, but leaned forward to look in
particular at a silver jet banked rakishly on its plastic
stand.

"I'm afraid those aren't very good, Deb," Don said.
"I was just a little kid when I made them."

"You were thirteen, Donald," his mother said. "You
built them the summer you had your appendectomy."

"This one is especially nice," Debbie said. "It's a
B-Forty Seven, isn't it, Don?"

"Uh hm. Would you like to have it?"

"Oh—I—are you sure—"

"It doesn't amount to much, but I'd like you to have
it if you want it."

It was the first thing Don had ever given her. It was
only a ninety-eight-cent plastic airplane, but somehow
it seemed much more than that. "I would like very
much to have it, Don," Debbie said soberly. "I'll put
it on my desk in the office. Thank you." Debbie
reached for it carefully and took it with her to the
couch. She sat beside her cousin, holding the model in

her lap.

Then, as Robert came in with two small cups of black coffee for Don's parents, Mrs. Carver smiled sweetly and said, "Donald, you must designate which of your remaining models I may have. A mother attaches a certain sentimental value to such things, you know."

"You can have all three of them, Mom," Don gestured magnaminously, "even the one with the broken tail—and the footballs, too, if you want them."

"The broken tail doesn't matter," his mother replied gently. "I shall treasure it fully as much as the others."

"Anybody want to watch T.V.?" Don asked. "Lance Cannon is on." Lance Cannon was a T.V. jet pilot. But before anyone could reply, door chimes sounded in the hallway, and a few seconds later, Robert appeared to announce the Winthrops.

Robert needn't have bothered, however, for Kay was right behind him. "Hi, everyone!" Kay went directly to Don's mother and embraced her. Then she turned, brimming with good humor, to recognize the others.

Mrs. Carver acted very surprised to see the Winthrops; a bit too surprised, Debbie thought, while scolding herself for being so suspicious.

After Shayna was introduced, Kay said, "You can't

imagine how surprised I was to see *you*, Debbie! We simply couldn't fathom whose car that was in the drive!"

It was as flimsy as it could be, and Debbie could not down the conviction that the Winthrop's arrival had been pre-arranged. "We just had dinner, Kay," she said and, smiling toward her hostess, added, "A very marvelous dinner."

"Scrumptious!" Shayna elaborated.

Mr. Winthrop, a big, friendly man with a deep voice, took over. "I tried to prevent these two from barging in here like this," he boomed, "but they consider your house a second home, Milt!" Kay's father seemed a strange mate for his sparrow-like wife. And his extroverted character—which he shared with his daughter— seemed even stranger for a banker.

"Just a little informal dinner, Win," Mr. Carver replied. "We're happy to have you."

"Why don't us four old fogies get up a game of bridge?" Mr. Winthrop demanded. "Expect the kids would be glad to be rid of us."

Mr. Carver looked uncertainly at his wife. She laughed. "You know very well, Win, how the prospect of bridge tempts me!" She hesitated. "However, I shouldn't want Deborah and Shayna to feel that I had deserted them—still, I'm sure that the young people would be quite happy without us." Mrs. Carver placed a hand on Debbie's shoulder. "Or do I dare leave my son alone with three such lovely girls?"

"We four will get along fine, Mrs. Carver."

"I am sure of it, my dear. Kay darling, promise me that you will see to it that Deborah and Shayna enjoy themselves."

"Clara, you run along to your bridge game," Kay purred. "If things get dull in here, we'll set fire to the place!"

Sickening, Debbie thought.

But Don's mother evidently thought it very funny. "We will be in the library if anyone wants us."

"Mrs. Carver," Debbie said, "Shayna and I want to thank you and Mr. Carver for the lovely dinner now, so as not to interrupt your game later." Debbie was pleased that she could speak so calmly when she was seething inside.

"Yes," Shayna seconded, "it was awfully sweet of you to ask Debbie and me."

"We've enjoyed having you both. Now if you want anything at all, just ask Robert for it. Come, Milton."

As the older people filed out, Don's father paused at the door to look back at Debbie. It appeared for a second or two that he would speak, but he lowered his eyes and followed the others down the hallway.

The next hour was a torturous one. Don was ill at ease and defensive. Debbie hid her anger beneath a minimum of formal conversation. Kay was her usual bubbly self, oblivious to everything except her own desires. When Don again suggested turning on the T.V., she made her own preference known at once.

When the western faded to its inevitable ending in time for the rash of nine o'clock commercials, Debbie whispered to her cousin, "Don't you think we'd better go, Shayne?"

Shayna looked doubtfully at Kay. "Whatever you say."

Don made a half-hearted objection, then accompanied them down the hall. Kay stayed behind, exploring new channels on the T.V. set.

The library door was open, so Debbie and Shayna put their heads inside and waved.

"Good night, Deborah—Shayna!" Mrs. Carver called. "Do come again soon!" The others waved too, and said good night.

Don escorted them to the Chevy and opened the car door. He seemed forlorn and unhappy, Debbie noted as she got in, placing the model in the seat beside her.

"Good night, Don." She put out her hand and he took it eagerly.

"Good night, Deb. I'm sorry the Winthrops kind of broke in; they didn't mean to spoil anything."

"It wasn't your fault. Besides, it's been a lovely evening."

"I was proud of you," he said.

"I'm glad." She withdrew her hand and started the engine. "And, Don—?"

"Yes, Deb?"

"Please don't set fire to the place!" Debbie eased out the clutch pedal and drove away, smiling. Don was still standing in the drive, looking after them, when they turned into the street.

CHAPTER XVII

At eight o'clock Friday, Debbie and Shayna took the car and drove to town for the mail; that is, the mail was their excuse for going to town. They went directly to Pearson's, where they bought the morning *Journal*, and hurried to a booth to look for the story of the girls' record flight.

They had determined before they sat down that it wasn't on the front page. Then they began to doubt that it was on *any* page. Well, Mr. Carver had said that it was "tentatively" scheduled for that morning. Maybe he had decided to save it for Sunday, after all. Or maybe it would be in tonight's edition.

"I don't see why Mr. Goodman went to so much trouble," Shayna said resentfully, "if he didn't think the story would be printed!"

Mr. Tibbs approached the booth, wiping his glasses

with a paper napkin. "If you girls are looking for your names in the paper, they're on the sports page."

Debbie had that section. She threshed through it impatiently. "I don't see it, Mr. Tibbs."

"Down there in the corner. See?" He pointed.

Shayna got up to look over Debbie's shoulder. "Is that all of it? Why, it's only four lines!"

Debbie read it aloud: "Miss Debbie Mills, seventeen-year-old daughter of Ben Mills, Twin Lakes airport operator, announced yesterday that she had established a woman's distance record for two-place gliders. Her passenger was Miss Shayna Todd, of Lawton, Oklahoma, who is visiting Miss Mills here."

Debbie's eyes stung. Why, she couldn't believe it!

Shayna flounced angrily back into her seat. "Some newspaper!"

Debbie carefully put the paper together again, folded it, then solemnly offered it to the pharmacist. "May I have my nickel back, please?"

Mr. Tibbs laughed as Debbie slid from the booth. "It does seem like the *Journal's* got a grudge against you, doesn't it?"

"I suppose we expected too much, Mr. Tibbs. Ready, Shane?"

Outside, Debbie noted that the feathery cirrus clouds

high above were being replaced by lower and thicker alto-cumulus. "It's going to rain this evening," she remarked as they got in the car. Inane—but she had to say something. Her heart felt as if it bulged against her rib cage.

Shayna lifted her shoulders indifferently. "Where to now—the post office?"

"I'd like to go by Sammie Goodman's house for a minute. Her dad has been so nice, I don't want him to think I blame him for anything." Maybe he'd have an explanation, Debbie thought.

The Goodmans' new home was on the north edge of town. Their Rambler station wagon was in the driveway, and Mr. Goodman, in old clothes, was watering the recently planted lawn as Debbie and Shayna drove up.

"Hi, Mr. Goodman! This must be your day off. Is Sammie home?" Debbie was climbing out of the car.

"She was in the back yard a few minutes ago. How are you girls this morning?"

"Fine, thanks," they both said as they went around the house.

Sammie, barefoot and in shorts, lay in a hammock staring at the clouds. She swung her feet to the ground as she heard her visitors close the gate. "Hi."

"Hi, Sammie." Debbie grinned, thinking Shayna never had a chance to talk any more.

"I hope you didn't come to apologize or anything like that!" Sammie blurted. "Dad says it wasn't your fault!"

"Apologize?" Debbie repeated. "For what?"

"Because Dad quit his job. That's why you came, isn't it?"

Debbie was appalled. "You mean he quit his job because—oh, Sammie, I—I—"

"I told you, Debbie, *you* couldn't help it! Daddy had four columns, with pictures and everything, about your record flight. Mr. Carver called about midnight and killed it. My dad says it would have been front page stuff if it had been about anyone but you, so he quit."

"I feel terrible!" Debbie said. "I wouldn't have—" She could hardly keep the tears back. Sammie had been so nice, and so had her dad. Why, this was awful.

"I keep telling you, Debbie, my dad doesn't blame you! He says a paper either has integrity or it hasn't, and that life is too short to work for one that hasn't."

"But what will you do? Your dad is a newspaperman, and there aren't any other papers here." Debbie swallowed the big hard lump in her throat.

"We're going to sell our home and move to Wichita or some place."

"You just bought it!"

Sammie turned her head away, her dark eyes suddenly moist. "We can buy another one."

"Oh, Sammie—" Debbie started, but had to stop, too choked to go on. She was crushed. The fact that the Goodmans did not blame her made it harder, not easier to accept. No matter what they said, she *was* to blame. If she had bowed to Mrs. Carver's wishes to start with, quit seeing Don, this would not have happened!

"I'll see you later, Sammie," Debbie said in a low voice. She could hardly wait to get home. Her dad would straighten her out.

"'Bye." Sammie did not look up.

Returning to the car, Debbie was relieved to see that Mr. Goodman had gone inside. It would have been hard to face him. She and Shayna stopped at the post office, then drove back to the airport. They didn't talk much. Debbie's heart was too full. Her thoughts went round and round.

It was fifteen minutes before nine o'clock as they pulled onto the apron and parked beside Betty Clarke's blue Volkswagon. The Cub was there, so Debbie expected to find her dad and Betty in the office. But she didn't. She located them finally on the south side of the hangar. They were hitting golf balls and laughing with the delight of children.

Shayna had gone to the apartment, so Debbie stood for a moment at the corner of the hangar, watching them. It had been a long time since she had heard her dad laugh that way.

A few seconds later she turned, sensing movement behind her. George was rolling the Fairchild outside. "What's Dad going to do with that, George?"

"Don's going to use it for his cross-country, Miss Debbie. Your dad wants him to go right away. Weather people predict rain this evening."

Debbie walked beside George and followed him around while he fueled and checked the red monoplane. At last she told him about Mr. Goodman. Bless old George, she could always talk to him.

The old mechanic did not reply at once. He stepped inside to his work bench, returning with a bottle of Windex and a soft cloth. Cleaning the windshield, he said, "Paul Goodman is right. It wasn't your fault. He did right to quit, too. He's too good a man to be wasted on Milt Carver's personal propaganda sheet!"

"George, I just *know* Mr. Carver would have printed that story! It was Mrs. Carver who wouldn't allow it!"

"Milt's just as guilty as she is for goin' along with her!" George finished the windshield, then took off his glasses and gave them a squirt of Windex. "Milt's goin' to be mighty sorry he lost Paul Goodman," he concluded.

"The Goodmans just moved into their home last week!" Debbie wailed. "I'm absolutely *sick*, George!"

"Now, Miss Debbie, you—" He was interrupted by the sound of an approaching car. It was Don.

Debbie saw at once that Don was troubled. He parked beside the other cars and got out, unsmiling. "Hi," he said. He reached for Debbie's hand as he walked up to them. It was an unusual gesture under the circumstances and, Debbie thought, there was something about it that hinted at a need for reassurance. She was reminded of a little boy seeking help and not knowing how to ask for it.

"I see that you have the plane ready, George," he said.

"Ready as a puppy's tail wag!" the old mechanic replied.

"Okay. Let's go into the office, Deb, so I can get the nine-fifteen weather."

Debbie's dad and Betty followed them inside. Greetings were exchanged; then Don spread an air chart on the desk to plan his trip while Debbie's father watched.

But Don's mind was clearly not focused on his task. He made two mistakes in calculating headings, and one of the check points he chose was unacceptable. Then, estimating his fuel needs, he forgot to include the forty-five-minute reserve supply that Debbie's dad always insisted upon.

Debbie saw that her father was puzzled. Ordinarily, Don's arithmetic was flawless. "Do you feel all right this morning, Don?" he asked.

"Sure, Mr. Mills."

"Get plenty of sleep last night?"

"Well—yes."

Debbie's father was thoughtful for a few seconds. He turned to Betty Clarke. "If you'll check with George to see if the Cub has been gassed, we'll go ahead with your lesson in a few minutes, Betty."

"Roger, Ben." Betty went out.

"Wait!" Debbie called. "I'll go with you." Debbie knew that her dad wanted to talk with Don alone; the Cub had been ready for hours.

CHAPTER XVIII

As Debbie re-entered the office, Don was standing at the window, hands clasped behind him, staring across the fields where George had rolled the Fairchild back into the hangar. He neither turned nor spoke.

She waited for a few seconds, then went to his side. "Don," she said softly, "tell me what is troubling you."

He reached for her hand, but made no reply.

"You were there when I needed help—remember? Maybe I can at least give you some moral support." Her love rushed out to him. Oh, how she wanted to help.

He released her hand and began pacing the floor in agitation. "It's mostly just personal stuff, in my own family, Deb. You can't do anything." He sat down heavily in the swivel chair.

"You don't blame Dad for cancelling your flight,

do you?"

"I guess not—he doesn't want one of his planes busted up."

"He was thinking of you, not the plane, and you know it!"

Don leaned forward, gripping the arms of the chairs. "Now there *you* go! Why is everyone so belligerent?"

Debbie refused to flare back this time. "I was merely setting the record straight," she said evenly. "It's about time someone did—about a lot of things."

"Brother! You can put *that* to music!"

"I said I wanted to help, Don, not fight," she replied gently.

He bit the corner of his mouth and sat back with eyes downcast. It was as much of an apology as she could expect. Debbie knew by now that apologies were rare from a Carver.

Then he looked at her again, and she could see the hurt in his eyes. "Deb, I've never heard my parents argue—I mean really argue and shout at each other—as they did last night. It went on until two this morning!"

Debbie sat on the leather couch and gazed down at her hands clasped in her lap, waiting for him to go on.

"Their rooms are at the other end of the hall from

mine, and I didn't know what it was all about. But Mr. Goodman quit this morning, and one of the printers told me it was because Dad killed a story about you."

Debbie raised her eyes to his. It was out now. A showdown was unavoidable. "Don," she said quietly, "I think that you have suspected for some time how your mother feels about me."

He stared at her for long seconds, anguish on his handsome features. He got to his feet again and returned to the window. "It just *can't* be that way, Deb!"

"But it *is* that way! Refusing to face it is not going to change it!"

He whirled to face her. "Do you think I could choose between you and Mom? I tell you I won't do it. *I love you both!*"

Debbie's heart leaped up, then grew quite still. He'd said it. He meant it. Oh, bless him, she had to help him.

Debbie was surprised that her voice could sound so steady when her heart was having "a fly-in" all its own.

"I'm not asking you to choose between us, Don. I'm asking you to recognize the simple truth! You can't make a thing go away by denying that it exists. You've got to examine it and weigh it and think about it and then, if you can find the courage, do whatever your conscience tells you to do about it!"

"Don't you think I've tried that? I tell you, Deb, there's nothing I can do. I can't control other people's thoughts."

She went to him and took his hands. "Have you ever told your mother that you are in love with me?" Her lips let the words out lovingly, tasting the beauty of the expression.

"Gosh, Deb, people ought to understand *some* things without having them spelled out."

"Not *that*, Don. After all, you had never told *me* until a few seconds ago! But if your mother knew that you had asked me to wait for you until you graduate from the Academy, it might make a difference—that is, if you *do* want me to wait for you."

"Sure I do, Deb," he replied softly. "I thought that was also understood."

Careful now; don't rush him. She bit her tongue and tried to say the right thing. "Girls don't take things like that for granted, Don. Nor has your mother any way of knowing unless you tell her."

"Well, maybe you are right," he said slowly. "Maybe I haven't held up my end very well. Guess I'd better talk to Mom."

She put his hands behind her neck and managed a smile. "Now don't be—I mean, try to see her side, too. This isn't a question of choosing her or me, but of helping her to see that I want the same things for you that she does."

"Well, one trouble is Kay. If Mom weren't so sold on her, things would be easier."

"What you mean is that it hurts you to disappoint your mother. Of course it does. But that disappointment has been there, waiting for her, from the start, because you wouldn't pick Kay even if I didn't exist. The kind of man who wants to 'go out there a little way,'" Debbie glanced upward through the window into the deep blue of space, "is not the kind of man who can be bought for the price of an airplane. This is a thing your mother should take pride in, rather than suffer disappointment." Debbie took his hands from the side of her neck and stepped back to smile at him through misty eyes.

Don mustered a smile, too. "You make me sound noble. But I don't feel very noble."

"Go talk to your mother," she whispered, "then call me." Again her heart came up into her eyes and looked out.

He raised his arms, and she stepped into them, her

heart throbbing there against his heart, and for a few seconds, at least, there were no problems at all.

After Don had gone, Shayna came into the office. She and Debbie fidgeted for the next forty-five minutes. They spoke desultorily, and the Carvers were not mentioned.

At last the phone rang. But it wasn't Don calling— it was his mother. Mrs. Carver hesitated for several seconds after identifying herself, and when she spoke, her voice was low, devoid of its usual sureness. "Deborah, will you come to my home? I should like to talk with you."

"Yes, Mrs. Carver. I'll leave at once."

"Thank you. I'll be waiting." Debbie heard the little click as Mrs. Carver put the receiver back in its cradle. She replaced her telephone receiver and turned to Shayna, trying to keep her voice from cracking.

"Don's mother wants to see me, Shayne. I think I'd better go alone." Then she began to shake. She couldn't control her voice, let alone her legs.

"Sure, Debbie, I understand—and I'll say a prayer for you, too."

Ten minutes later, Robert answered Debbie's ring and led her into the library. Don's mother was there, immaculate as usual, and seemingly calm. She offered

Debbie a chair, then waited until Robert closed the door before speaking again. Don was nowhere in evidence.

"Deborah, I should like to thank you for coming," she said quietly.

"I was anxious to come, Mrs. Carver."

Don's mother smoothed her left eyebrow with the heel of her hand. "My son has just informed me that he wishes to become engaged to you. I want you to know that I have given my consent."

Debbie was certain that it was the most difficult sentence Clara Carver had ever uttered. Significantly, too, Debbie thought, Don's mother had chosen the word "consent" rather than "blessing."

Debbie remained silent for long seconds. It occurred to her that she had won, but it was not the victory for which she had fought. Somehow she had won the prize while losing the contest. At last she said quietly, "Thank you, Mrs. Carver. I hope that you and I will be friends."

"Of course we shall, Deborah."

Debbie waited uncomfortably. It did not seem proper for her to excuse herself and leave, yet what was there to say in that atmosphere of armed truce?

"There is one thing that I should like to ask you,

Deborah. I ask that you refrain from any act or suggestion that may tend to discourage Donald's plans to complete his education and attend the Academy. If you truly care for him, you will do nothing to harm the brilliant future that lies ahead of him."

Debbie had to swallow hard. She was finding it more and more difficult to control her resentment. "What did you expect that I would do to harm Don, Mrs. Carver?"

The older woman looked at her guardedly. "When Donald returned for the car this morning, he went to his room for a time. I later discovered that he had packed a bag and concealed it beneath his bed." Mrs. Carver's tone indicated that this should be explanation enough.

"I'm afraid I don't understand." Debbie frowned.

"I see," Don's mother said with an air of finality. "So you disclaim any knowledge of it, is that correct?"

"I know absolutely nothing about why Don should pack a suitcase, or why it is connected with me in any way, Mrs. Carver. Don didn't mention going away to me. Did you ask him about it?" Debbie had never felt more puzzled.

"No," Mrs. Carver said coldly. "In fairness, I wanted to give you the opportunity to confess, to be honest with me. I had hoped that you would—especially after having received my consent to your engagement."

Debbie's anger flared. "I have been honest with you, Mrs. Carver. I know nothing whatsoever of Don packing—" Debbie did not finish, for Mrs. Carver arose from her chair and went out into the hall.

She was back almost at once. "I have summoned Donald. I shall ask him in your presence."

A small nerve in the back of Debbie's neck began to jump. The queen had summoned!

Don entered a few seconds later. He waited until his mother resumed her seat, then placed a chair beside Debbie. He said nothing as he sat down, but his manner was that of one prepared for anything.

"Donald, would you care to offer *your* explanation of the piece of luggage packed and waiting in your room?"

It was all Debbie could do, as Don glanced at her, to keep from protesting this injustice; Mrs. Carver's emphasis clearly hinted that Debbie's version had already been heard.

Don, of course, knew differently. "Mom, I don't see how you could have anyone's version except mine. Debbie couldn't have known anything about it!"

"Oh? What reason would you have to leave here alone?"

Don did not hesitate. "Because you and Dad quarrelled on my account, and because of the way you feel about Debbie."

"What of your future, Donald? What of the Academy?"

Don compressed his lips stubbornly, refusing to say more.

His mother stared at him with fear in her eyes. "There's no *need* to leave! I have agreed to your engagement!"

He shook his head. "It's no good this way. I'll get a job so I can support Deb away from here."

His mother covered her face with her hands as Debbie slipped from the chair to stand before him. "Don, there is no reason for you to leave. It isn't you, but me, who has caused the trouble and misunderstanding."

"There's no use talking, Deb. I'm not going to the Academy with things like they are now!"

"That attitude is not worthy of you, Don. You're a bigger person than that! The Academy has been your dream, and your parents' dream for you—your whole future is at stake!"

"You were in that dream, too, Deb," he said quietly.

Debbie's eyes stung. Oh, how she loved him. But she had to be strong.

"I'm glad; but it all goes together, Don. If you leave, or give up the Academy, I can't see you again." Her voice broke.

He leaped to his feet. "Do you realize what you're saying?"

"Of course I do! I care too deeply for you to destroy you! Nor could there possibly be any happiness for us together, living with the knowledge that, but for me, you could have done far more with your life! I'm going to help you realize your dream—or I'll say goodbye, a final goodbye, here and now, in this room!" She had to swallow the sob in her throat.

He stared at her in silence for a long time. At last he said, "All right, Deb, if that's the way you feel about it." He took her hands. "I'll stay and see it through."

As Don made this quiet pledge, his mother came to her feet. "Deborah," she said, her voice choked with emotion, "I've cruelly misjudged you! I—I—" She faltered, then held out her arms to Debbie. She stepped back a second later, dabbing her eyes with a monogrammed handkerchief. "We *will* be friends, won't we, Debbie?"

Debbie fumbled for her own handkerchief. "Golly, *yes*, Mrs. Carver!"

Don joyfully hugged them both. "Now that I've finally got you two on the same team, just watch ol' Don go, boy!"

When Mr. Carver barged in fifteen minutes later, he found the three of them laughing over cokes and cookies—a situation which plainly surprised Don's father. He came to an uncertain halt; then, apparently convinced that the scene was real, he grinned. "Er—hello."

"Whatever are you doing home in mid-morning, Milton?"

His grin widened. "To tell the truth, Clara, I was going to make a slightly corny speech."

"You made one at two a.m. this morning, dear." His wife smiled. "A very good one; and I have thought about it quite a lot."

"So I see!" He expanded visibly. "I'm glad it got such good results!"

Mrs. Carver slipped Debbie a secret smile and said nothing.

Don's father sat down with them. "So, Debbie, you think that you can wait four years for this space-happy son of ours? Four years is a long time!"

Debbie nodded agreement. "But think how proud all of us will be, Mr. Carver."

Don's father chuckled. "I'm pretty proud right now. Has he asked you to become engaged yet?"

Debbie nodded, beaming.

"Fine. That gives Clara and me an excuse to offer you an engagement gift! Now I've got something in mind, but first, I'll ask if there's anything you particularly want?"

"Golly, Mr. Carver, I don't know. I—"

"Don't be hesitant, Debbie," Mrs. Carver put in. "This generous mood of Milton's probably won't last!"

"You hush, Clara," he said good-naturedly. "Anything at all, Debbie; just name it."

"There *is* one—" Debbie began tentatively. "Did you say anything?"

Mr. Carver nodded smugly. "I'll bet you're thinking of the same thing I was going to suggest."

Debbie doubted that, and she paused, afraid that her request would be improper. But she was convinced that Don's dad was a fair man, so she gulped and said, "Would you talk to Mr. Goodman again?"

It caught him unaware. Mr. Carver sobered for a second, then chuckled again. "Knowing you, I should have expected something like that! Sure, Debbie, I'll try to get Paul back. I was looking for an excuse to go after him anyway!"

"If you were going to ask Mr. Goodman anyway, Dad," Don injected, "you should give Debbie another choice."

"One to a customer, Son," his father replied with mock seriousness. "Now it's your turn; what would you like?"

Don's answer was ready. "Cast your vote in the council to renew Mr. Mills' lease!"

His dad threw up his hands and laughed aloud at this. "Okay! Okay! Everybody's asking for someone else's wish! That was supposed to be Debbie's request! You were supposed to ask for an airplane!"

Don looked cautiously at his father. "Would I have gotten it?"

Mr. Carver pretended to consider. "Well, I have a hunch that Winthrop will be happy to get his investment back from that Cessna. I thought I might just take it off his hands."

Don leaped to his feet with a whoop of joy. He grabbed his mother, lifting her from her chair and swinging her around in a ridiculous dance. She seemed not to mind the loss of her dignity, and was laughing with him as he released her.

"C'mon, everyone!" Don called. "Let's all go to the airport and watch Mr. Mills check me out in my new plane!"

His mother sought refuge on the divan, still laughing. "You and Debbie run along, Donald! Your father and I have had quite enough excitement for the present!"

Don shook his father's hand and pecked his mother on the forehead. As he and Debbie went out hand in hand, his dad called after them, "Don't forget to tell Ben about the lease!"

"Roger, Dad!"

The news Debbie and Don took to the airport occasioned a modest celebration there. Then, after lunch, it rained. But the rain didn't matter because, as Debbie exclaimed to Don as they were coming out of Rosen's Jewelry Store, "It's the most beautiful rain I ever saw!" Of course, this observation may have been influenced by the most beautiful diamond she had ever seen, now reposing in Don's pocket.

It was a stone that seemed almost indecently large to Debbie; but Mr. Rosen said that Mrs. Carver had called and specified that the ring should be "adequate."

On the following Monday, the day before Shayna had to leave, the first fly-in breakfast was held and was a huge success. More than forty planes were there, and Mr. Goodman devoted nearly half of the *Journal's* front page to the event.

One of the highlights of the occasion was the announcement—kept secret by Debbie's dad until the last moment—that Debbie had been named a member of the United States Soaring Team.